Richard Screamed "Look Out!

Oh no no no—" And he started to run although it had scarcely happened yet.

At the head of the chute a small child with a bunch of flowers in his hand suddenly popped up from the ditch and started across the road just as Charley appeared halfway around the turn in a fast, controlled slide.

The child stopped, rooted to the center of the road. Richard, running, saw it happen now, saw Charley correct the slide to avoid hitting the child, turning the wheel in the only direction he could, saw the machine whip out of the controlled drift and hurtle out over the edge of the mountainside.

Saw the bright, blue car glint in the sun as it turned slowly end over end in mid-air, then land far down the side of the ravine.

Richard ran and fell several times on the steep, rocky hillside, his lungs aching painfully, and then Felice grabbed him by the arm and hung on. "Don't go down there," Felice said, his voice shaking. "Oh, Holy Mary, Mother of Jesus . . . It is better not to see—there is nothing you can do—it is better not to see." Felice made a noise like a hurt animal and stumbled back to the bent tree and retched.

Richard stood there and watched. He saw the ambulance halt when it could go no further. Then the stretcher bearers ran ahead, clawing their way up the rocky slope to where Charley lay in his bright blue coveralls, like a bundle of dirty laundry.

MY MISTRESS, DEATH

ROBERT SPAFFORD

WILDSIDE PRESS

Chapter One

IN THE TWILIGHT she came down the long worn stone stairway and crossed the silent square to the fountain, which was really only an iron pipe in the shape of a gorgon's head, from whose mouth the clear cold water of the mountains ran endlessly. The girl put down a tall copper vessel so the stream would flow into it and stood leaning against the wall of what had been the castle moat a long time ago.

From where she waited, she could see down the steep valley to the sea, thirteen hundred feet below her. The light was fading rapidly now, but the white dusty road that winnowed from the village down to the valley floor, doubling back on itself a hundred times, was easily visible in the gloom. Nothing moved on the road. At her feet, the water splashed pleasantly in the copper gourd, but she did not look to see how full it was, for the changing sound would tell her.

She was seventeen, and tall, as many Italians of the north are tall, but she was as dark as a Sicilian, and this was because her father had come from Messina, after casually killing a man in a knife fight. She had long black hair, and the incomparable posture which is the result of carrying very heavy loads balanced on the head from childhood. Her feet were bare and dirty from the dust in the square, but her limbs were straight and fine, and she looked like a young madonna. Her name was Ghita, which meant Margherita-Luisa-Teresa Pilbo.

The gourd was nearly full now. Still she watched the empty road, thinking: I could wait here for thee, seeing the dust cloud on the sea road which thy machine would cause, but I must not. For when thee comes, I must be clean and sweet for thee, and there would not be enough time for everything that must be done. So I must deny myself the pleasure of watching the road. For thy sake, Massimo . . . She took a rag from her pocket, twisted it into a rope and formed it into a ring, which she placed on top of her head. Then, bending from the waist, she lifted the gourd easily, although it weighed fully sixty pounds, and set it securely on her head.

As she started up the long steps again she was unaware of the weight she bore, or of the suppertime sounds which squeezed through the closed shutters of each window she passed. The house her father had left her was one of the highest on the cliffside, and was level with the great terrace of the towering castle, around which the village was wrapped.

Massimo comes tonight, she was thinking, moving in the slow sure manner that scarcely rippled the surface of the water in the vessel. Tonight he will be here in San Gregorio, and I will hear his machine in the square, and then he will be coming up these very steps, running, although he should not run, and then he will bring his little-boy face smiling into my house, this house that has not known love for a long time. . . . She pushed open the door and went into the one room and put the gourd on the stove, in which the fire still burned hot from the cooking of supper.

It was a very nice house, Ghita thought, and it was very clean; there was none cleaner in San Gregorio, and many dirtier. Naturally she owned chickens, but these were cooped on the roof with the pigeons, and not permitted in the house. Sometimes she thought it would be very nice to have a pig of one's own, but each time she visited her neighbors, the Picelli family who owned four pigs, she changed her mind. No, it was better this way, and though she had no perfume, there was the rosewater, and the no-smell of everything clean. She wondered about the women Massimo must know in Rome and Milan and Turin and even in Paris, and although she had never smelled one of these women, she had seen their pictures in the journals and was sure they must smell very strongly of expensive perfume; wondering about it, she said aloud: "That has nothing to do with me. Only that he comes back to me."

While she waited for the water to heat, she took from the cabinet the dress Massimo had brought her in the spring. It was white silk jersey and as soft as skin, Massimo had said, his black eyes enormous with wonder and excitement—"Like the soft skin on the inside of thy thighs," he had said breathlessly; and "Feel it! Then touch thyself just here . . ." Proudly he told her how much it had cost in a fine shop in Milan, and he laughed at her expression of disbelief, for this was nothing to what he was going to do for her. Soon he was going to be very rich and she would come to live in the cities and wear such clothes every day, and jewels, and she would be more elegant than any of the other women, even the noble ones, or the foreign women always to be seen on the Via Veneto in Rome itself. His boundless imagination stirred her hardly at all; she listened to him brag and was happy because he was happy, but she did not really believe in any of it, for San Gregorio was her world and she was not tempted beyond it.

Still, the white dress was an undeniable fact. She spread it out carefully on the bed, and went back to the cabinet for her shoes. These she had made herself, tiny moccasins of white kid, and much more practical than the shoes with the ridiculous heels which Massimo brought with the dress. Those shoes had insane heels, very tall and with stones like diamonds and not much else. She could not stand on them even when the strings were tied about her ankles. "How can one stand only on the balls of the feet?" she asked him. "A foot is not meant to be bent out of shape this way. Thee has been cheated. Take them back and demand thy money." But Massimo had only laughed and knelt before her to remove the shoes and kiss the bruised toes, and then she had forgotten all about the shoes until he had gone away again.

The water was steaming. Ghita dragged the washtub into the center of the room and emptied into it the simmering contents of the copper vessel. Now it was suddenly quite dark and she lighted the oil lamp and set it on the table, and with one motion stripped herself of the cheap black cotton dress which was her only garment. With one tentative toe she tested the water; it was too hot. Resting her foot on the edge of the tub, Ghita first braided her hair and then wound the heavy plaits into a crown atop her head, and then stepped slowly into the water. It was still so hot she felt as if the tub were full of nettles, but she thought that if she could stand it, it would make her skin pink all over, which would be a pleasant surprise for Massimo, who has once told her that the women of northern Europe did not have the tanned, olive skin of Italian women; it was, he swore, still amazed at the memory of it, pink and white as the sunrise over Monti del Beleri. The discomfort was acute, but Ghita bore it.

Later she pulled shut the one window which looked at the castle and across the roofs of the town toward the valley. With the lamp lighted, the window gave back her reflection, as she rubbed herself dry. There were no curtains or shutters on the window because Ghita had no wish to keep out the sun or the moon, nor did modesty make any such requirements, for the house was too high on the cliff for her to be observed, unless someone were watching from the castle terrace, which was unlikely. The *gran signore* of San Gregorio, Il Principe Vittorio Sacriponti, prince, patron and proprietor of San Gregorio by an inheritance six hundred years old, would not be in residence in his castle until tomorrow. What she saw in the crooked window panes was good; she was firm and straight, and in full bloom. It was a strong body, made for work and childbearing, but if it was to be used for neither of those things, and only for love, well—it was made for that, too. Massimo had seen many women of the world, rich, noble, famous, and yet he always regarded her with awe when she undressed, saying softly that she was incomparable, his eyes showing that he spoke the truth.

A faint sound swept up on the valley breeze; Ghita snatched the windows open. Silence for a moment in the distance; she ignored the wireless of Signor Pecci in the *trattoria* in the street behind the square, and the barking of half the dogs in the village as the moon showed itself behind Monti di Beleri. Faustini was beating his wife again, and getting as much as he gave, from the curses and shouts that floated across from the next house . . . Ghita listened not to the village, but the valley, and the bright white ribbon of the road glowed in the moonlight and although nothing moved on it within sight, there was a great dust cloud all the way from the *autostrada* junction up to where the road disappeared for several kilometers behind the hills. The noise came then, a distant sound, flat, blatting, like a stick drawn along a paling fence, and then a descending whine, echoing between the mountains. Ghita's heart beat with sudden violence. She left the window and pulled the white dress over her head; the bodice was like a peasant blouse, worn low around the shoulders and tight across the breasts. She pulled on the white kid slippers. Then, very carefully, in order not to spill any, she dragged the washtub to the far corner of the room where a trench set in the stone floor formed a drain to the outside. Slowly she tipped the tub until it was empty, rinsed it with water from a pitcher, and stood it upside down over the drain.

The sound was coming much more frequently now, and louder each time, the staccato reverberations like the gunfire that had been heard in these mountains only a few years back; Ghita had a moment of panic, wondering whether to leave her hair in the crown of braids, or to comb it out full, but after a moment she decided to leave it. It was, she thought, the way the women of the cities would wear it, and anyway, she knew what pleasure it gave Massimo to undo it and brush it out with his clever, sensitive hands. There was nothing more for her to do in preparation. The supper had been ready for an hour and was warm in the oven, and the wine stood cold in the earthenware jar. She would not stand in the window, watching to see the machine roar up the last climbing curve into the Piazza di San Gregorio. She knew that the sound of his coming was eagerly awaited by others, for Massimo was the great and growing hero of the village, and his admirers would swarm from the *albergo* and the *trattorias*, from the houses under the moat and the shops in the piazza and the houses on the cliff. They would swarm around him, laughing and shaking his hand and trying to slap him on the back and wishing him luck, and Ghita did not want him that way, shared into so many little bits that there was not much of him for anyone. She wanted him whole and complete unto herself, and so she would not watch at the window. Ghita sat down in the straight chair beside the table. She smoothed her skirt, and then sat absolutely still, hands loosely clasped in her lap, knees and feet together, to wait for Massimo. She looked serene, but inside she was calling to him: *O amore*, hurry, hurry; already the hot waves are rolling through me for thee, I am your house and your home and the door is open.

Chapter Two

WHEN THE ROAD finally led out of the dark ravines and circled the last mountain that obscured San Gregorio at the head of the valley, Massimo said loudly over the noise of the engine, *"Ecco!"*

"For Christ's sake, back off, will you?" Richard Delgard said.

"Che cosa?" Massimo turned his attention from the road to look at Richard in surprise.

"Watch the road!" Richard said sharply, and repeated it in Italian. They were coming into a blind curve with the rev counter showing forty-eight hundred in third gear, which meant eighty kilometers—almost fifty miles per hour, even allowing for the wheel spin on the loose, fine sand of the road; miles or kilometers, it was too fast. Richard braced himself with one hand on the door handle and the other clutching the grab handle on the dashboard. It was a right-hand drive car, so Richard's seat was on the inside of the turn, and if the car looked as if it were going over the edge, he swore to himself that he was going to jump. They were almost into the turn now and Massimo's hands and feet worked so fast they were almost invisible.

The revs went up to six thousand and they were in second gear now and Massimo's left foot had moved from the clutch to the brake, but was not pressing it; the right foot was steady on the accelerator and his hands held the wheel lightly, while with a forefinger he tickled the head-light switch so that the flickering beam would warn cyclist or donkey cart, truck or pedestrian, if any or all were just beyond the curve of the hillside. The car was drifting now as they entered the sweeping bend, the rear end trying to slide out to the unprotected edge of the cliff, and the spinning wheels trying to go where the front wheels pointed along the radius of the turn. Richard had an insane urge to jerk at the wheel and the handbrake, although he knew by training and experience such an act would be fatal for them both. The rear wheels were riding the very rim of the canyon now and there was nothing below the edge except the near-vertical mountainside with an occasional

10

olive tree that might slow their plunge, but not much. He waited for the slight lurch that would mean the right rear wheel was spinning in free space, and the door handle was already in the open position. They were committed to the curve now, and the four-wheel drift of the car seemed perfectly calculated to the arc of the turn; Massimo kept the engine accelerating under full power. If they did not hit a rock or a ditch or a soft spot or a slight nibbling away of the canyon rim, they would get around. The curve seemed endless to Richard, in whom fear was so great it filled his throat; all the muscles of his great body ached in spasm, and he was suddenly soaked with sweat. . . . They came out of the curve and, feeling the car straighten, Richard realized his eyes had been closed. He opened them and relaxed a little and said in Italian, "Slow down, you nameless son of a whore." But he thought in English, "You crazy son of a bitch, it's the last time I'll ever ride with you."

Massimo was smiling, but he slowed down a little. "It is for the village," he explained softly in his own tongue. "That is the first curve they can see clearly. But it is nothing to be nervous about. I know every inch of that curve, every inch of every kilometer of this road. I walked it enough when I was a boy." He looked at Richard and stopped smiling. "Ricardo, forgive me. Was it very bad?"

"Yes," Richard said. "It was the worst. I was going to jump."

"So bad, truly?"

"Truly," Richard said. "It is usually bad in the passenger seat, but sometimes it is almost unbearable."

"I am sorry." He said it sincerely, but he did not sound convinced. The American watched him sideways, wondering what went on in Massimo's head. Massimo had the hands of an artist, or a magician, or both; he was undersized and he looked underfed, but you didn't often think about it because there was lightning in his eyes.

Richard said, "You have never felt it?"

"No," said Massimo. "I have heard about it, but I have not felt it."

"I don't mean only like this," Richard said. "I don't mean just riding with racing drivers who have an ability you know and respect. The other times—when you have to go for a Sunday drive with some lunkhead who doesn't know the clutch from the brake. Or some woman."

"No," said Massimo, and he sounded regretful. "Once at Monza, when we were practicing for the *Gran Premio,* this man came up and introduced himself and asked me to come for a check-ride with him for a few laps. He is from a very noble family, very rich, and I heard later that he takes drugs and is also thought to be a little crazy in the bargain. But he has more money than the Church, and he wants to be a racing driver—he has seventeen sports cars in his palace in Rome, they said, and he drives up and down the Via Veneto wearing his crash helmet and goggles and the Pirelli coveralls . . . Well, the prince had a lovely new Ferrari. I got in and we started off. He was the worst driver I ever saw; he was not a driver at all; it was a crime to let him touch such an automobile. A man who would treat a machine like that would molest children."

Now the road bent in a great sweep to the right around the end of the valley, climbing the last two kilometers to the village. San Gregorio was simply a vertical extension of a small mountain that looked like an inverted ice cream cone, with the graceful spires of the castle at the apex.

"My God," Richard lapsed into English, "it's strictly Walt Disney. Don't try to tell me it's real."

Massimo, not understanding, went on in Italian about the molester of children. "Everything should have blown up, the way he started off. Ten thousand revs? Who knows! We left rubber for thirty meters, and then he missed the gear change going into the Lesmo Corner. He was on the wrong line and too fast for him and he lost his nerve. And then he lifted his foot off the gas and hit the brake." Massimo coughed suddenly and spat out the window. "He was going to kill himself and probably me, too."

"You felt it then?" Richard said.

"No," Massimo answered. "I did not want to be killed in company with this degenerate, you understand. But it was not the bad feeling you speak about. I was excited, inside. I had never been in such a bad position. On a right-hand drive it is, of course, almost impossible for the passenger to get at the accelerator—"

"Putting it mildly."

"—so I punched him in his groin. That took his feet off the pedals and his hands off the wheel, and I yanked on the hand throttle until I thought it had come out by the roots. The power came on and we began to drift but it is very hard to steer accurately from such a position. You understand?"

"I have an idea," Richard said dryly.

"It is a very strange feeling to be in such a situation. Very strange, but not bad. Only exciting. Maybe like fighting bulls. Or making love to a strange woman."

"You didn't crash after all?"

Massimo laughed. "Oh, yes, of course, Ricardo. We crashed beautifully. I expected that. But we did not crash where this eater of carrion would have crashed us. We got past the ditch and the trees before going off the road and rolling over in an open field. We were very lucky, because the ditch would have killed us, certainly. Truly we were lucky."

"You weren't hurt at all?"

"No," Massimo said, and added apologetically, "not in the crash. It was very strange. I pulled him out of the car—it was completely written off, you understand—and I waited while he vomited on the grass. Then, suddenly, this noble prince found his bravery. He became very brave. He broke my jaw and two ribs for crashing his car."

"A noble fellow, indeed," Richard said. "Some time you'll kill yourself for the lack of the feeling of fear."

"You believe this, Ricardo?"

"I believe it," Richard said flatly. "The bad feeling comes when there is true danger, if you are a man. If you are not a man, the bad feeling can come long before the danger is true. It is man's natural protective instinct."

"This worries me," Massimo said. "Why do I not know the bad feeling?"

"We have a saying," Richard told him, "that only a fool denies he is afraid, and only an idiot denies it with truth."

Softly Massimo asked, "Dost thee think I am idiot or fool, beloved Ricardo?"

"Don't ask stupid questions." He grinned at Massimo and added in English, "You're out of this world."

"Che?"

"It doesn't translate," Richard said. "Just say you belong to the devil."

Massimo liked that, but he crossed himself, just the same.

The crowd in the piazza scattered frantically as the car slid around the last turn past the fountain and swapped ends in a calculated skid that brought the car up short before the entrance to the Albergo Bersaglieri.

"Neat, not gaudy," Richard said. Understanding nothing but the tone of cynical admiration, Massimo threw him a flashing grin and climbed out of the car, to be smothered in the collective embrace of the villagers. A very large man with a fantastic comic-opera mustache came out of the hotel with arms outstretched.

"*Bambino mio*," he said again and again in a great bass voice, walking through the crowd as though they did not exist, to fold Massimo in his arms and kiss him repeatedly on the cheeks. Richard unfolded himself from his seat and stood on the cobbled piazza, stretching his aching muscles. Across the square, from the roof of the hotel to the steeple of the church, extended a rope, holding a cloth banner which proclaimed: Welcome To Our Hero Son Massimo in huge letters, adding underneath as if in apologetic afterthought: "and to all the other participants and spectators at the Gran Premio di San Gregorio."

Massimo came back through the crowd, arm-in-arm with the big man to where Richard waited. "My uncle," said Massimo, "thee is no longer the only giant in San Gregorio. Behold my friend, Ricardo Delgard. Is he not an entire army in himself?"

Uncle Fausto held out his huge hand. "*Come sta, Ricardo?*"

"*Va bene, grazie, signore,*" Richard said, taking the hand, anticipating the pressure. The two men smiled and no sign of the struggle showed in their faces. Uncle Fausto was incredibly strong, but Richard knew he was putting all he had into the handclasp, so he met it only with equal strength, because it would be tactless to shame Uncle Fausto in this manner.

The big Italian looked momentarily surprised, and then he smiled. "Thee must be one of my own get, Ricardo." He looked down at Massimo. "Where found you this monster? Surely he comes from the mountains of the north, although the accent—"

"Americano," Massimo said.

"Truly?" said Uncle Fausto.

"My grandfather's name was Delaguardi; he was born in the Piemonte."

"Ah, that is better," said Uncle Fausto. "He is Italian, then. Come inside, we will have a Strega."

Massimo said, "Only a very small one, Uncle. I am expected."

"Women must wait," Uncle Fausto said calmly. "It does not do to let them think they are important." He ushered them into the room which opened onto the piazza. It was a rough, vaulted room, like a cave, which served as lobby, dining room, office and bar. Uncle Fausto went behind the counter and set out the bottle of Strega and three glasses.

Now in the unshaded light Massimo's face looked pinched. Beneath his deep sunburn, the olive skin looked almost green, and his great eyes were deep in his head and there were dark circles beneath them. In this moment of repose, as he waited for the drinks to be poured, Massimo was just another undersized Italian with Brilliantined black hair and a badly cut suit, totally indistinguishable from millions of his race. Richard looked away, because he did not want to see Massimo like that, and because it made him even more ashamed of his own blatant health and strength. He looked at Uncle Fausto as the drinks were pushed toward them, and saw that the old Italian knew.

Massimo picked up his glass, and with the action he seemed to re-energize himself. "Call it, Uncle," he said.

"To the homecoming," Uncle Fausto said.

"Yes, that is good. To the homecoming."

Richard raised his glass. "The homecoming."

They drank. Massimo put his glass down quickly and began to cough. At first he coughed lightly, carefully. It began to take control of him and the coughs became a terrible thing of retching and gasping for air; he went down on his knees against the bar with his handkerchief covering the lower half of his face. Richard had watched this before, and because there was nothing to be done, he felt sick and looked out the window onto the piazza. Uncle Fausto came around the bar with a towel and a glass of water, murmuring soft words in the mountain patois which Richard did not understand. The old man gently took the handkerchief away from Massimo and pressed the towel to his mouth. Massimo's face had turned very red, but now it was ashen, and he was not coughing so much. Uncle Fausto made him sip the water, and while Massimo gasped over it, the old man said over his shoulder to Richard: "It is the fever of the lungs. You know of this?"

"Yes," Richard said, not looking.

"He has had it for a long time, but now it is very bad."

"Yes," Richard said.

"You have been with him long, Ricardo?"

"Six months only, my uncle," Richard said.

"You have seen it as bad as this?" Uncle Fausto persisted.

. . . What good does it do to talk about it? Richard thought. There was the time at Zandvoort when Massimo was leading the *Grand Prix*, even ahead of the Ferrari team, and suddenly he had stopped on the back leg of the course. Richard had seen the car right afterward, because he went in then as relief driver, and the cockpit of the car was a mess, although they tried to mop it out hurriedly . . . "About the same," Richard said.

Massimo stood up uncertainly and he kept his back to them as he mopped his face with the towel. "Another Strega, Uncle," he said in a whisper.

"Is it wise?" asked Uncle Fausto.

"It is necessary," Massimo said with more strength.

Without expression, they watched him drink the liquor carefully, and when he put the empty glass on the counter, with only a stifled tremor in his thin chest, they both knew Massimo had reasserted his dominance. He had challenged the Strega as he would always challenge every risk that presented itself, and once more he had won. One day, Richard thought, you will meet the Big Risk, and because you do not have the bad feeling to protect you from this rashness, you will challenge the Big Risk too . . .

"I am late," Massimo said, "for that which improves with waiting, but only up to a certain point. Prepare thy biggest bed, Uncle Fausto, for Ricardo. Better still, put two beds together so he may sleep crossways—otherwise his head and feet will drag on the floor. Pleasant dreams, Ricardo."

"You're not sleeping here?" Richard asked.

"Ho," said Massimo, winking at Uncle Fausto, "listen to him. No, Ricardo, thee must be happy without me tonight."

"Beat it, runt," Richard said. "You're too thin for me."

Massimo laughed and went out the door and across the piazza, through the crowd of villagers, smiling and shaking his head when they tried to detain him for conversation; and then Richard and Uncle Fausto, standing at the window, watched him start up the steep steps, taking the first three or four with dignity because he was being watched, until suddenly impelled by his perpetual need for speed, he began to run up the steps three at a time.

"Let us have a quiet drink together, Ricardo."

"Yes, thank you, *padrone*."

Richard abruptly felt tired and dried out, and the tenseness that always preceded a race had already begun in him, so that he knew he could not get to sleep easily. He did not enjoy drinking very much, but it was either that or the sleeping pills, and the effect of the latter stayed with him too long.

They had two drinks apiece, and then Uncle Fausto went out and got into the car with Richard and there was a moment of embarrassment for the American because the driver's seat was adjusted for Massimo, so that it was only with great difficulty that Richard could get his legs under the wheel and shut the door. The villagers waited critically while Richard swore silently and tried to get his feet in position on the pedals. He started the engine, and blipped the throttle violently for the benefit of the public, and pulled around the corner of the hotel into the tiny alley leading into the garage of the hotel which would be used as team headquarters for the race.

It was a small, poorly lighted garage with a hard-packed dirt floor, but it was the best in San Gregorio. They left enough room for the three racing cars of the team, which were expected in the morning, and put out the lights and locked the doors with a medieval key a foot long.

"It will be clear in the morning," Uncle Fausto said, looking at the sky, "but very likely it will rain in the afternoon."

"Then we'll practice in the morning."

"And in the afternoon, in the rain, if it rains."

"Why?"

"Because the race will be run of an afternoon, and here at this season it is very likely to rain in the afternoon."

"All right," Richard said. He had never been in San Gregorio before, but he knew the course diagram by heart and he had seen many photographs of it. About half of the two-mile course went through the narrow streets and alleys of the village, with eight right-angle or hairpin turns, and the rest was a long climbing and then diving crescent around the flank of the mountain. That last section was dirt, like the road up from the valley, and the rest of it was either tarred surface or cobblestones and badly worn stone paving blocks, some of which dated to Roman times, and which were forbidden by the government to be removed or repaired. If it rained there would be many cars bent up against the houses and hillsides, Richard thought, and I do not like it very much. Let's be honest, He said to himself, you don't like it at all.

Chapter Three

I ɪ ᴛʜᴇ ᴍᴏʀɴɪɴɢ it was very hot in the piazza, and there was no shade anywhere except in front of the *trattoria* of Signor Guerrerra, which boasted an ancient olive tree. There was not a breath of wind, and the sun burned down on the dusty leaves, but beneath the canopy of the olive tree it was cool, and here were clustered the little tables and chairs of the coffee shop.

Richard had been up since six. Uncle Fausto had pushed two double beds together for him, and he had slept across them, so that even Richard's six-feet-four had for once had plenty of space. But the bed was lumpy, and he had slept fitfully, without losing the tenseness, anxious for the morning to come. And now, for two hours, he had been walking around the course. He had walked slowly and with concentration, noting the road surfaces, the ditches and culverts, the radius of turns at the street corners, and the places where the steps of the houses projected out into the already narrow alleys. He had a dependable and nearly photographic memory for detail, and as he sat in the shade of the olive tree, drinking the black bitter coffee and eating a sweet roll, he drew a remarkably exact map of the course on the white marble tabletop, marking the danger points, and the estimated cutoff points where you would have to shut down and stand on the brakes in preparation for each corner. When he was finished, it looked very impressive and it looked frightening, too, because there were some very bad places.

Looking up from the diagram, he squinted across the bleached square to the humpbacked stone bridge spanning the deep ravine which divided the main part of the village from the houses which had overflowed to the immediately adjoining hill. You would be coming fast down the hill on the other side, down into a dip, then up over the bridge, and if you were coming as fast as you would have to, to be in the race seriously, you would be airborne for several seconds as you came over the top—a few seconds and thirty or forty feet. When you got the wheels back on the road you would have run out of bridge altogether, which

19

would not matter except that thirty feet further on there was a house with solid stone walls. All right, Richard thought, all you have to do is be in a turn when you land, in order to miss that house. That will be fun, boy, he said to himself, yes sirree, bub, some fun. He saw the proprietor watching him and he called out, *"Per favore, signore! Ancora un espresso e un panettino."*

"Subito, signore."

Even in the shade, Richard was beginning to perspire, and he supposed it was from the coffee. He sat waiting for Signor Guerrerra to bring another coffee and bun. From inside the *trattoria,* which was simply a vault hollowed out of the solid rock of the hillside, came the sound of milk being forced by steam pressure out of the big nickel urn into the coffee. The proprietor came outside with the tray of coffee and cake in one hand and a carafe of white wine in the other.

"The wine of the district, *signore."*

Richard didn't want wine at this hour, but he understood that it was being offered as a courtesy.

"I would be grateful," Richard said, "if you would join me."

"I am honored," Signor Guerrerra said. "And I have brought out two glasses."

He filled them both, and raised his, but he did not sit down.

"Salute."

The wine was light and dry and very cold, and drinking it, Richard realized he was very thirsty and was beginning to enjoy himself. "It is a proud wine, truly," he said.

"It is only a little wine," said the proprietor modestly, "but for a little wine it's a relative giant."

"What you say is true," Richard said.

"Have another. It is my pleasure."

"I shouldn't," Richard said. "I'm supposed to start practicing in an hour."

At the point of refilling the glasses, the proprietor said, "You are the partner of Massimo?"

"One of them," Richard said, thinking: You're nothing but a lousy relief driver, a spare, a fifth wheel, and unless Massimo, or Felice, or Giorgio drop dead, get drunk, or shot by an irate husband, you won't even get a chance to drive in the race . . . "We're on the same team."

Signor Guerrerra refilled the glasses. "There is nothing

to worry about, then. The racing machines have not even arrived yet. I have been watching for the van, but it has not appeared."

They drank, gazing out across the sunbaked piazza. Up to now there was no indication of activity out of the normal routine of this ancient hill village, except for the limp banner stretched from the church steeple to the hotel's roof. Most of the male villagers worked the surrounding farms and olive groves and had already left by this hour, but there was a steady procession of women and children crossing the piazza to the fountain in the castle wall.

"It is a beautiful village, and very peaceful," Richard said.

"It is very peaceful," the proprietor agreed. "For three hundred and sixty-two days of the year it is as peaceful as the grave. But for the other three days of the fiesta of the race, all hell breaks loose." He emptied his glass. "To-night you will see, when the fiesta begins."

He excused himself and went back inside, leaving the carafe on the table. Richard understood that the racing teams brought a certain spirit of carnival with them when they descended on a town, but in his experience there was little of the chaos at which Signor Guerrerṛa had darkly hinted.

A piercing whistle stabbed at him from high on the hillside. It was an imperative and mocking sound and Richard knew that it could be only Massimo. He got up and went out from under the olive tree to where he could see the hillside houses. In the open window stood Massimo in his underwear. Richard waved, and Massimo saw him and waved back, then held his hands out the window with the fingers splayed. It meant either ten times, or ten minutes; Richard didn't know which, but he waved again and when Massimo disappeared from the window, Richard returned to the shady table.

For a while he thought about Massimo without coming to any new conclusions, but only thinking that they liked each other very much and got along excellently, probably because they were not in competition with each other in one single thing. Although Massimo was David to Richard's Goliath, there was nothing that Massimo envied him, neither his incredible physique or his money, his education or his background. If Massimo didn't kill himself, he would be champion of the world, probably next year and no later than the year after, and compared to that, there was nothing else of importance.

The girl came down off the hillside steps with the copper gourd on her head, and walked with slow grace, barefooted, across the hot cobblestones toward the fountain. Richard had never seen her, but he knew it was Ghita. Even the cheap black dress could not disguise the lines of her body; he found himself holding his breath as she passed near the *trattoria* to take advantage of the coolness of the cobbles under the olive tree. My God, he thought in astonishment, I'm seeing things. He had expected Massimo's girl to be pretty, in the style that Italians prefer in their women, but he had not imagined this rare, authentic madonna beauty. She went out of sight around the corner by the fountain, and Richard let out his breath, slowly, suddenly aware of the sweat on his face. The carafe still felt cold and he poured another glassful, and sat waiting for her to come back.

A flock of geese shambled erratically across the cobbles, complaining about their hot feet; Richard watched them idly, then abruptly sat up as the geese began to scream in alarm and made abortive takeoffs in all directions. A moment later the threat appeared from the fountain corner; a black Bentley Continental slid silently to a halt before the hotel.

Richard had not wanted to see the Bentley in San Gregorio, and at Monza the week before he had been sure it would not come here. Diana had said she wanted to go back to London, and Geoffrey had quite naturally concurred. The season had really finished with Monza, and San Gregorio was of course only a second-rate event, which the Ferrari works team, and Maserati's, would not likely dignify with their presence. Apparently it was harder for Goeffrey to say no to a race than to his wife, because here they were in the hot sun of the piazza of San Gregorio.   •

His first impulse was to pay the bill and start walking out of town, because he didn't think he could face Diana after Monza. It would not be easy to face Geoffrey either, and this part of it he hated as much as anything, because he had no real reason to feel guilty before Geoffrey. He had done nothing to harm Geoffrey. That's enough, he said to himself, don't go any further with that; just leave it alone.

He watched them get out of the car and stretch, and then Uncle Fausto came out of the hotel and they all shook hands and even from this distance, Richard could see that Uncle Fausto was tremendously impressed with Diana, casually polite with Geoffrey and coldly formal to Hans von Lutzow. He could not hear what was being said, but he watched the two men pull the luggage out of the Bentley and start inside, while Diana received the homage of Uncle Fausto. After a moment, Uncle Fausto turned and pointed toward the *trattoria* and Diana looked that way, and waved, and started diagonally across the square.

Watching her come toward him, he felt his muscles tighten the way they do when you are expecting a punch. He sat braced, waiting for her, wishing he could feel hatred, or contempt, and knowing that he was kidding himself.

She was very blonde, with unbelievably dark eyebrows, and very dark-blue eyes, and that slim elegance of figure which can be far more exciting than the ripe voluptuousness which reaches its perfection in bodies like that of the girl of Massimo. Diana walked lazily and surely across the uneven pavement of the piazza, as though the whole world were waiting for her.

"Hello, there," she called out in her brisk, impersonal voice. Richard waited until she had arrived at the table, then he stood up slowly, and they shook hands in the European fashion.

"Hello, Diana."

"Hello, darling," she said, and sat down. "Must say you don't look a damned bit happy to see me."

"I don't think I am," Richard said.

"What are you drinking?" she demanded, and at the same time picked up the carafe and poured a glassful. "Cheers." She tasted it. "Not bad. Not bad at all. Do ask for a decent-sized glass for me, and a *gespritz*."

"This isn't Germany," he said carefully. "Will a siphon do?"

"Don't be bloody tiresome, Dicky. It's too early in the morning."

"Oh, stop it, for Christ's sake," he said in anger.

"That's better, darling," Diana said. "Let's not fight yet."

"I don't want to fight at all."

"That's a love. Nor do I."

"Then why did you come?"

She opened her eyes wide, looking straight at him, and her voice was small and hurt. As if it explained everything, she said, "Geoffrey."

He said nothing. Diana became very clipped. "You don't believe me?"

"No."

She emptied the wine glass, set it carefully back on the table and turned her direct glance on him. What looked like genuine pain showed in her eyes, but Richard no longer trusted her.

"Is this what love is like, Dicky?" she asked unsteadily.

"If it is," he said harshly, "I don't want any more of it."

She stared at him for a long moment. "You have the coldest, cruelest eyes, you know."

"Stop it, Diana. It doesn't do any good."

"But—"

"Shut up about it," Richard said, leaning across the table.

"Give me a cigarette," Diana said. She sat back in the chair and crossed her legs. She wore no stockings, and the skin of her legs and arms and throat was a deep tan against the white skirt and the starchy, white transparent blouse; he could see the white satin brassiere as clearly as though she were wearing mosquito netting. "Did you ask for my glass?"

Glad to have something to do, he lighted a cigarette for her and then went away from the table into the cool dampness of the cave and brought back a tall water glass. The fact of using his muscles made him feel better, but as he returned to the table he was uncomfortably aware that he was walking with his chest out and his shoulders back. Normally he moved loosely in an effort to look smaller.

Diana let her admiration parade across her face. "Don't walk on the balls of your feet. I know you're beautiful."

With sudden savagery, Richard said, "Why don't you get the hell out of here? Why don't you take Geoffrey and that—kraut—the hell off to London? Haven't you done enough harm?"

Fascinated, Diana said, "Please hold my hand, Dicky."

"Can't you take a hint?" he said in utter exasperation.

"Can," she said, "but jolly well won't. I love you, Dicky."

"Sure," he said, filling her glass.

"I do, you know," she said earnestly. "Hell's own amount."

"Sure. Drink the wine."

"You said you loved me."

"I was lying."

"Not likely. No more than I was. Oh, I'm a bloody awful liar about a lot of things, but not that. I couldn't even lie to Geoffrey when I married him. He knew I didn't love him."

He didn't want to say it. "And Von Lutzow?"

"Don't be silly, darling."

"You slept with him."

She put down her glass. "What a swinish thing to say!"

"It's true, isn't it?"

"Of course," she said, "but you don't have to be a swine about it."

"Oh, God," Richard said.

"And anyway, it was your fault." But she looked ready to forgive him.

Richard sighed heavily. He knew what she meant, but her motivations were peculiarly her own and he would never understand them. It was only a week ago at Monza that Richard knew he was hopelessly in love with her, and for the moment he had believed she loved him. She had wanted to go away with him, then and there, and when Richard had refused because of Geoffrey, she had the next day gone away for the weekend in Rome with Hans von Lutzow. Clearly, it was Richard's fault.

He had been drinking wine without noticing it, and now he felt it all at once. It was no longer cool under the olive tree, and it crossed his mind that they were going to have overheating troubles with the cars; following that line, he wondered if Angelo had ordered the larger radiators fitted. "What did you say?"

"You've gone away," Diana repeated.

"Yes," he said heavily, "I have."

She said softly, "It means nothing to you?"

"What, specifically?"

"That I want you, most awfully."

"You've got Von Lutzow," he said roughly. He didn't care what happened now; it would be fine if he tore everything apart and did away with it.

"You are a beast," Diana said.

"When you let Von Lutzow touch you, I was finished," Richard said.

"But we'd never even begun," she said passionately. "Do you think I could have looked at that swine if you and I had ever been together?"

"He's a swine, but good enough for you?" Richard said.

"He's a swine," she said furiously, "but he's a man."

"Obviously."

"Oh, God," she pounded her fists on her knees. "Talk about British superiority! You Americans, with your old school ties—"

"Americans don't have old school ties—"

"Oh, but you have! And you're wrapped up in yours, Dicky, like a cocoon."

He stood up, feeling as though he had been pounded all over. She wouldn't look at him, but her hand reached out. He couldn't bear to have her touch him. "Dicky, darling," she said in a very small voice.

"You know I hate being called Dicky."

"Dick," she said, "I'm a rotten bitch, and I can't help it. You know I can't help it, don't you, darling?"

He knew she was weeping although he didn't look at her, and he thought: how wonderful to be able to let it all out that way . . . in a minute she'll be all fresh and clean and new again. But I can't cry, so I'll keep on carrying the load, slung over my shoulder by my old school tie.

"I guess you can't," he said.

"Isn't there anything we can do about it?"

"Probably not," he said. He touched her hair absently and her whole body stiffened. "With a cornball like me, there's only one way it could have worked. The way I said that night. Only to tell Geoffrey honestly, and beforehand, not afterwards." He paused, then added slowly, "I don't think you wanted to divorce Geoffrey. Or wanted to marry me."

"Oh, I do, I do!" she said despairingly.

As though he hadn't heard, Richard went on: "But you thought that was provincial thinking on my part. Well, you showed your contempt for my viewpoint. You were very effective about— Diana," he said in sudden anguish, "how could you have let that son of—"

She stood up, very close to him, and there was a fierce intensity in the dark eyes. "You walked out on me," she said. "Remember? You left me standing there in the garden, and stalked off all noble and righteous, and I stood there crying because I couldn't go back into the party and face anyone, and then Hans came. He wasn't noble or righteous or even gentle. He knew what he wanted, and I didn't care when he kissed me because at least it was good to be· wanted, but after a while I told him not to be such an ass, and he knocked me down. Yes, he did, and from the moment I felt his fist I didn't care what happened, because nothing was any good, anyway—"

"Stop it!" he breathed. "Stop it!" He was sick with fury. "I'm going to take that dirty bastard apart—is that what you want?"

Diana laughed. The tears were still streaming down her face, but she made the sound of laughter, saying, "Oh, Dicky, Dicky, what rotten timing! What's the good of being masterful now? You should have thought of it that night in the garden."

Richard walked away from her, out into the blinding sun, without destination, but before he realized the lack, one was provided for him by the huge racing van which turned the corner at that moment and shuddered to a halt in front of the *albergo* with an ear-slitting squeal of brakes and a geyser of steam escaping from the radiator cap.

Chapter Four

Massimo lay on the bed in Ghita's house, eating an apple while he waited for her to come back from the fountain with the water for his bath. The night had gone very well, and he was content, and there was no need to dwell on it. He felt wonderful, and he wondered if he dared have a cigarette, but decided against it. The trouble with the coughing had only happened once during the night but Ghita had given him a glass of olive oil to drink, and it was not as bad a spell as that of the moment in the *albergo*. The doctors in Torino had been very stern with him, but he did not really believe them; all the same, with the season coming to a close with this race, he might go to Sestriere and stay in bed for a few weeks. One doctor had said that six months flat on his back might give him a couple of years, but the other doctor had said two years in bed or Massimo would never see his twenty-fourth birthday. He thought about this with unaffected detachment; they meant well, of course, but doctors always exaggerated. He would be twenty-four in the spring, and it seemed a very ripe age to him.

Campione del mondo, he thought. It was a very nice sound, and of course, with luck, it is only a matter of time. Of luck and the machines. Don't forget the machines, friend; one doesn't become champion on foot.

He thought about the race. It was not an important race in itself, but it was very important for Massimo, because it was the end of Massimo's first big season. He had not won a single important Formula II race, but then he had been driving with inferior machinery against the official factory teams of Ferrari and Maserati, whose resources and facilities guaranteed that their racing machines were better prepared than those of the private entries. But San Gregorio did not attract them this year, and the privately owned four-cylinder Ferraris of the Scuderia Barzio would be competing only with teams whose machines were certainly no better prepared. Massimo was primarily interested in the speed, power, and reliability of the entries in the race, because the respective

28

abilities of the drivers gave him little concern. He did not understand why it was so, but when he was at the wheel of any given machine, it went around the course faster than it did for any other driver. The racing journalists said he saved seconds on corners; but lost them at the pits. Well, he thought, he had studied the technique of the great ones and could not see where his cornering style differed from theirs, except that it was faster. As for losing seconds in the pits, a racing car was meant to be raced, and more often than once he had been leading even from Ascari and Villoresi and Fariña, only to blow up the engine and have to retire. But now it was going to be different, because the great Signor Enzo Ferrari, himself, had spoken to him after Naples, and there was a good possibility of a berth on the factory team. If Massimo did well here on Sunday . . . He could see himself as teammate of Alberto the Master, the present world's champion. Alberto the perfectionist, who drove faster and with fewer mistakes than any other. If the machines were equal, he would beat Alberto Ascari next year.

Massimo threw the apple core out the window and brushed off his fingers on the sheet. He wished Ghita would hurry with the water, because he was impatient now with anything but the machines, although he had not yet heard the racing vans. Well, he would go down and have a coffee with Ricardo. He was sorry about Ricardo. It was a shame that Ricardo was such a great monster. With the big cars, the four-and-a-half-liter cars, it had not made so much difference, and he knew that Ricardo had done very well in America with the big ones.

But the two-liter cars were another matter. They were so light, their power-to-weight ratio so carefully calculated, that an extra hundred pounds or more added precious seconds to the laps. It was like dragging an anchor, Massimo thought—and that's not all. The cockpits aren't big enough for Ricardo, and his legs get cramped, and that's when you begin to make mistakes. It was very bad, a dirty shame, because Ricardo had it. Even though he talked about the bad feeling, he had tremendous courage and determination, and when he was in a car that fitted him, his style was as precise as Farina's. But he will never get there, Massimo thought sadly, and he deserves it so much more than the others, particularly since he is an

American. They are very good at many things, the Americans, and even unbeatable at Indianapolis, but they lack something in *Grand Prix* racing; it is a question of temperament, and the Americans have not the required temperament to be among the great ones. Yet, he said to himself, Ricardo is American and he has it to a definite degree. But then, he remembered, the grandfather was a Piemontese, which probably explains it. All the same, it is too bad.

He got up and went to the window, and looked toward the fountain, but his attention was diverted by the black Bentley in front of the hotel. Massimo whistled silently. *La contessa,* he thought, *molto, molto bella.* His glance swept the piazza. Ricardo was standing close to the Englishwoman, just under the edge of the olive tree. Even from here, Massimo could appreciate her. He did not approve of her for Ricardo, and he was glad she belonged to someone else, but still he could appreciate her. He knew something had happened between her and Ricardo at that party after Monza, but Ricardo had not spoken of it, and naturally, Massimo could not ask. But the matter of the German, Von Lutzow, was a donkey of a different tail. Everyone knew about that—at least everyone except Geoffrey Partingbridge. Massimo wondered if all English husbands were like Geoffrey, who seemed to take no notice of his wife's behavior. Perhaps it was because he was some kind of nobility, although, in Massimo's experience, it was not the way an Italian nobleman would react. If she were my wife, he thought, I would whip her in the street; but it is no concern of mine. He thought about her a moment more, wondering if it was true that she was very easy. Lupi claimed she was. Lupi claimed he made her last spring in Switzerland, just like *that*. But Lupi always claimed that, no matter what woman you mentioned. It was all in Lupi's head, Massimo decided, and there weren't as many women in the world as Lupi claimed he'd had. If a woman as much as said *buon giorno, signore,* to Lupi, by lunchtime he was absolutely certain he had seduced her, at her request. She doesn't look like that kind to me, Massimo thought, but on the other hand, it wouldn't do any harm to find out . . .

He saw Ricardo turn abruptly away from the Englishwoman and go almost unsteadily across the piazza, and

Massimo wondered in surprise if he could be drunk. He saw the woman sit down again at the table and he considered dressing, without waiting for his bath, and going down to speak to her. But then the racing van with the big letters of Scuderia Barzio in red on its sides lumbered, squealing and hissing, into the piazza, and Massimo postponed the matter of the Englishwoman in favor of the more important matters at hand.

He blew a piercing blast through his fingers. Ricardo didn't heed it this time, but down by the fountain, Ghita heard and looked up, just as she settled the heavy gourd on her head. Massimo waved his arms wildly at her to hurry, and she waved back. Crossing the square, she nearly collided with Ricardo, and had to reach up hastily to steady the gourd, and then resumed her unhurried pace, while Ricardo walked right through the group of mechanics standing around the van and plunged into the hotel.

Chapter Five

HANS VON LUTZOW was not in sight when Richard burst into the bar. It was so quiet inside, and dim after the blazing brilliance of the sun in the square, that Richard thought the room was empty. He stood there, uncertain and half blinded, not knowing what to do next, and then from a corner Geoffrey's diffident voice said, "Hello, old chap!"

Geoffrey was seated at a small table with the race regulations spread out in front of him and a small battered English-Italian dictionary in his hand. He was very thin and narrow-shouldered, and his face began with a pointed jaw and ran upward and outward in a triangle; he had curly blond hair, rather fuzzy, that stood straight out from the sides of his head, making him look curiously flattened on top. Richard had never known anyone like him, and he could think of no conceivable reason for Diana's having married him. Geoffrey never used three words if two would do, and when he did speak, it was always in a shy, flat tone, almost as though he were apologizing for venturing a comment. He was generally believed to be a magician with engines, and it was true that he did moderately well with his three racing cars, which he had largely designed and constructed himself, and the financing of which had, according to rumor, very nearly exhausted all those assets which were unentailed properties of the seventh Earl of Carnmoor, Geoffrey Partingbridge.

"D'you mind?" Geoffrey looked helplessly at the race regulations and waved the dictionary to indicate the futility of his labor.

"Where's your kraut friend?" Richard said.

"Bathroom."

"What?" Richard said.

"Upstairs," said Geoffrey. "Some bloody amoeba."

"What?" Richard said again, his anger gradually giving way to bewilderment.

"Dysentery. Rotten luck."

"Hans?"

Geoffrey nodded, and the reaction was too much for Richard. He had come in here intending to smash the German to a pulp, but how can you hit a man with his pants down? He began to laugh. Geoffrey looked at him mildly.

"Howling joke, what?"

Richard said, controlling his hilarity, "I—I wasn't exactly laughing at what you think."

"Oh."

"As a matter of fact, it isn't funny at all. If you've had it, you know."

"Can't say I have," Geoffrey said thoughtfully. "Leaves me short a driver, you know."

"You can pick up one all right. There're always half a dozen Italians hanging around in the hopes of getting a drive."

"Not much good, usually."

"Adriani's all right, and he said he was coming."

"No English."

"Well, you don't expect to find an English driver—"

"Mean Adriani can't speak English."

"Oh," Richard said, thinking, neither do you, Geoffrey, old chap. "Not much. He understands go faster and overtake and faster still—"

"Slow down?"

"No Italian knows what that means," Richard said.

"Wizard," Geoffrey said, the corners of his thin mouth twitching with all the amusement he ever showed. "D'you mind?" he said again.

For the next ten minutes, Richard translated the race regulations, while Geoffrey slumped over the table, staring vacantly at nothing, his mouth slightly open as though inhaling the words. When he had read it all, Richard folded the mimeographed sheets and put them on the table.

"Decent of you, Richard."

"Not at all," Richard said. "Do you know that I'm in love with your wife?"

"Rather!"

"You know it?"

"Oh, quite."

"Look, Geoffrey," Richard said uncomfortably, "do you understand what I'm saying, or are you wondering how many tire changes you'll have if it's this hot on race day?"

"Don't be upset about it, old boy."

"Doesn't it bother you?"

"Why? Tons of chaps are potty about Di."

He felt as though he was flailing against a feather mattress, and it made him say more than he had intended. "I want you to understand that there's been nothing—nothing—" He didn't know how to finish it.

"Then why mention it?"

"I want you to know it. You're a friend of mine." He was beginning to feel like a fool.

"Oh, quite."

"I want to marry her," Richard said; he hadn't intended to say that at all, and it stunned him to hear it.

In his faint voice, Geoffrey murmured, "I dare say."

"Will you give her a divorce?"

"She want one?"

Richard hesitated; then he said bluntly, "I'll be damned if I know."

Geoffrey looked at nothing for a while. Then, "I say, let me know, won't you?"

Richard started to answer automatically, then he shut his mouth and stood up, knowing that his face was very red.

"Sure," he said. "I'm sorry."

"Don't talk rot," Geoffrey said.

"Okay," Richard said, going to the door. Geoffrey sat where he was, staring at nothing.

When Richard came out of the hotel, the mechanics had already rolled two of the Ferraris down the planks to the ground, and were easing the third one out of the truck. The cars had been thoroughly overhauled since the last race, which was unusual, because the Scuderia Barzio had gone through a loaded schedule this year; several times they had had to pack the cars in the van, then drive like the wind to the next event, just barely getting on the starting grid in time for the flag. It wasn't fair to the cars or the drivers, but then, it was important to qualify for the starting money which the team collected for each car that managed to negotiate the first lap.

Signor Barzio, the owner and operator of the racing organization to which Richard and Massimo were contracted, had not arrived with the van. He had gone to Modena to take delivery of a new Ferrari America four-and-a-half-liter sedan, for use as his personal transport, and he would be bringing Felice and Giorgio, the other two team drivers, with him.

Massimo came across the square with his quick, light step, as they got the third red single-seater down off the planks. His wet black hair shone in the sun and water ran down his cheeks. He was grinning hugely as he came up to Richard and threw a punch at the big man's shoulder. *"Come sta, Ricardo?"* How's my monster this morning?"

"Hello, small dropping of a donkey," Richard said. "Did thee sleep well?"

"Well," said Massimo, "but not much. Hey! Pepino!" he called to the chief mechanic, "let's start up two of these coffee grinders. We want to slide a few corners."

"I can't hear you," said Pepino without looking around.

"Wind up the rubber bands, or whatever there is under the hood," Massimo said, grinning, watching Pepino's back. The chief mechanic maintained a superior silence. He had no sense of humor whatsoever regarding the racing machines, and any prolonged baiting by the drivers could put him in an insane rage.

"Lay off," Richard said. "Pepino, pay no attention to him. But it would be appreciated if you would start up the engines so we can begin practice."

Pepino straightened up. *"Scusi, signore."* He looked at his watch. "Official practice time does not begin until eleven and the *carabinieri* will not permit practice until the roads are closed to other traffic. Furthermore, Signor Barzio would not like practice to start before he gets here. Furthermore, even if he was here, and even if the *carabinieri* permitted, I would not send the machines out in this heat. That black one—" he pointed a wrench at Massimo—"would peel a set of tires, cook the plugs and melt the engine before he finished the first lap, unless he slid over the cliff first." He turned his back on them and told the mechanics to push the machines around into the hotel garage.

"He is right, of course," Massimo said seriously. "So we'll take the coupe. I will show you the course."

"I have seen the course," Richard said. "This morning. I walked it."

"What was your lap time?"

"Two hours, more or less."

"In the coupe it will be two minutes, more or less."

"Less I don't need," Richard said.

Hurt, Massimo said, "Thee prefers not to go with me?"

"Thee," said Richard, "has hit the nail on the tail. I don't want another ride like last night."

"Oh, that," Massimo said. "Don't worry, Ricardo. Nothing faster than a two-minute lap."

"The hell with that. I won't even be able to see the road at that speed, much less learn anything."

They went into the garage and got into the coupe. "All right, Ricardo, I'll take you around slowly two or three times; then you can get out."

As they crossed the piazza Richard looked toward the *trattoria,* but the tables beneath the olive tree were empty. Two more of the big vans were just coming in past the fountain, and already on several of the buildings facing the church, paper streamers were being strung up by the merchants.

Massimo turned into one of the winding streets that straggled downward from the square into the most crowded section of the village. He knew everyone, and he waved at them all, driving with one hand and blowing the horn at the same time. Goats and sheep and children and donkeys, women with water jugs or bundles of firewood on their heads, old men bent under mountainous bundles of cloth, or kitchen utensils, or wine barrels, jammed the alleys. The houses were so tall and close together, even overhanging in places, the sun could not reach the street, and it was shadowy in a way that did not seem real, and damply cool.

All at once they were out of the lower end of the town, crossing the bottom of the ravine, and climbing on the tarred road through the dappled shade of olive and eucalyptus, up the concave flank of neighboring Monti di Beleri. They were above the village now and above the tower of the castle itself, and again Richard had the feeling that none of this was true, that it was something imagined, or something remembered from a fairy tale of long ago.

Massimo drove fast, but well short of the limit, and the road was smooth and clear. The road curved constantly to the right and they were drifting so effortlessly that it was not obvious unless you watched the nose of the car, which was pointing out over the rim and not along the path of the car at all. Massimo sat back, perfectly relaxed, his hands light on the slim wooden rim of the steering wheel. Richard was enjoying it now, as much as he ever could as a passenger. He felt fine, because it was a pleasure to ride with Massimo like this.

They came down off the mountain toward the hump-backed bridge. They took a straight line through the S-curve of the bridge approach, clipping the weeds of the ditch on each side in turn, and Richard kept looking at the bridge as it got bigger and closer. He had begun to hate that bridge this morning when he first walked over it, but now the hate was a big thing inside him, because the bridge was too much for him . . .

"Brace thyself, Ricardo," Massimo said.

Richard's right hand already grasped the bottom of the seat frame, and now he bent his left arm over his head and pressed the forearm against the lightly padded top of the coupe.

They came onto the bridge, still accelerating. Massimo steered sharply to the left, and for a moment the nose moved in that direction, so that Richard thought they were going right through the stone railing; but Massimo opened the throttle and the rear wheels broke away and began to skid, shrieking in protest. Now he corrected the steering to the right, holding the skid so that the car progressed straight across the bridge toward the hump, although the car itself was pointed twenty degrees off the path it traveled. The tires suddenly went silent and they were in the air.

Richard closed his eyes, and almost at once there was a great crash, and a gigantic weight pressed him down in his seat and then tried to throw him up through the roof. When he touched the seat again he opened his eyes. The tires were screaming again, and now the engine sound rose above it as full power went on. Richard was dimly aware that they were broadsiding into the building beyond the bridge, and his muscles tightened at this anti-climax. Then, miraculously, the building had slithered past, and they were no longer moving sideways, but were headed straight down into the piazza, with Massimo braking with short, hard jabs at the pedal.

Richard unhooked his stiff fingers from the seat frame, vaguely aware that they were wet; he looked at them and saw he was bleeding badly. Massimo saw out of the corner of his eye, and stopped the car short. Richard was so shaken by the experience of the bridge that he sat there dumbly, looking at his fingers. It did not occur to Massimo that anyone was to blame except the 'unmentionable who had left a sharp edge on the bottom of that seat frame, and he cursed violently and comprehensively not only the criminal responsible, but his relatives, his neighbors, and his progeny. Richard opened the door with his other hand and started to get out. Massimo protested that he must drive him to the hotel, but Richard smiled vaguely and made a face to say that it was nothing, and walked off across the piazza. He heard the door slam, and the wheels spinning as the engine revved up again, and then the descending sound of the engine on the overrun, which meant that Massimo was heading down into the lower town to start another circuit of the course. Richard didn't look around; he kept walking across the rough paving stones, which felt very solid and reassuring underfoot.

Richard went into the hotel and started up to his room, but he saw Uncle Fausto coming out of the kitchen, so he went over to him and said, confidentially, and in English: "What this country needs is a good five-cent straitjacket."

Puzzled, but polite, Uncle Fausto held his peace. He smiled and Richard smiled and they both nodded with deep courtesy and then Richard went on up the stairs to bandage himself.

Chapter Six

THE CUT was not deep enough to worry about, but it was going to be uncomfortable to drive. He washed it and shook some sulfa powder from the can in his first-aid kit, and was awkwardly trying to bandage his right hand when the door opened and Diana came in.

"I'll do that," she said. She pushed him down into a chair by the window and unwrapped what he had started.

"Who told you?"

"You left a trail," Diana said. She looked at the cut, appeared satisfied, and commenced wrapping the bandage expertly.

"Very professional."

"Quite," she said. "Did literally tons of it during the war, you know."

"No," Richard said. "I didn't know. I know very little about you."

She tied the ends and tucked them under. It was very well done. "You hear lots, but you know little," Diana said. "Sounds almost profound, does it not?"

"That's about it," Richard said, flexing his fingers carefully. "Thanks very much."

"Don't mention it," Diana said, smiling.

He sensed that she was laughing at him, and he said coldly, "Of course, I shot off my face to Geoffrey."

"Yes, of course."

"He told you?"

"Simply assumed it, Dicky." She walked past him and stood looking out the window. "Geoffrey would die before he'd breach a confidence."

"Then," Richard said, "I guess the subject is closed."

"It doesn't have to be."

"You lost me on that last turn, Diana." He laughed shortly.

"What's funny?"

"I was just thinking that for two people who are supposed to be speaking the same language, we seem to spend a lot of time misunderstanding each other."

"Tell me anything you don't understand."

39

"I don't even know where to begin. You might look at me when we're talking."

"I've no manners," Diana said, turning. "Better?"

"Why did you lie to me earlier?"

"Lie?"

"Lie," he said flatly. "You've never had any intention of marrying me, have you?"

Diana looked like a hurt child. "I meant it—when I said it."

"How am I supposed to interpret that?"

Her eyes opened so wide that it made her look afraid of him. Accusingly she said, "You hate me!"

"I don't hate you at all," Richard said patiently. "But when you go into this act you irritate hell out of me."

"You do," she said. "You hate me. I can feel it."

He shook his head in exasperation. "You know more ways of evading an issue—"

"Why do you hate me, Dicky?"

"God damn it," he said, "so *I'm* on the defensive now. What have I got to be defensive about with you?"

"Because you wish you didn't love me."

"All right, I admit it," Richard said.

"And so you resent me."

He was appalled to discover that he wanted to hit her, and he had a faint suspicion that she expected him to. He said, "Let's skip the phony psychoanalysis. One thing at a time. You let me think you wanted to marry me. Why did you bother?"

She looked at him for a long moment, and then her glance wavered downward, tears filling her eyes. He waited, shrinking further into himself with each moment, moving away and away, so that in his mind's eye Diana grew steadily smaller.

Below the window in the piazza there was a regular procession of arrivals; trucks and passenger cars and even several of the road-equipped competition machines. Without thinking about it, he recognized most of them by the sounds, and here and there in the babble a familiar voice stood out. He was wasting time and emotion, and they could not be replenished like an empty fuel tank. "Let's go downstairs."

Still she said nothing, only sitting with her hands clenched in her lap. Richard turned away and started for the door.

"We're bad for each other, Dicky."

He waited.

She said, "We'd kill each other. It's very curious."

"Yes," he said heavily, "it's very curious, indeed."

"That's why, you know."

"You wouldn't care to explain?"

"Haven't I?"

"Maybe in English. Not in American."

She got up then and came to him; putting her arms as far around his neck as she could reach, Diana pulled him forward and kissed him on the mouth, hard, straining against his body. For a moment he was completely passive, then revulsion swept through him, because this was not the way he wanted her. Even her ready passion was suspect now. He pulled his head back.

Her face was naked, as he had seen it before, and each time it had disturbed him more, so that now he had the feeling he was being warned and challenged at the same time against looking deeper into her than anyone has a right to do. He did not know what he was seeing—perhaps her soul, if she had one, or whatever hides back behind the eyes—but he understood that a man could get lost there.

"Pull down the shades, baby. People are looking in."

She made one instinctive gesture toward the window, but he held her.

"Joke," Richard said.

She got it at once, and in that moment the shades came down, and it was safe, so he kissed her on his own terms. He kissed her so hard their teeth touched, bruising their lips. He released her and, unsteadily, she took a step back. Dazed, she said, "You hurt me."

"A minute ago that's what you wanted, wasn't it?"

There was a discreet knock on the door, and Angelo Barzio came in, his dark eyes bright with amusement. He was a stocky, hawk-faced man of forty-five, the product of the best tailor in Rome and a wife who was heiress to one of the most impressive fortunes in Italy. She was rich enough so that Angelo could indulge both his hobbies, which he described as motorcars that run very fast and women that don't run at all.

Angelo went directly to Diana and kissed her hand. *"Mes hommages, madame la contesse,"* he said. Then to Richard, he said in his soft, intimate voice, in almost unaccented English: "I heard Massimo tried to kill you."

"Nothing serious." Richard wiggled his fingers. "Diana just bandaged me up."

Angelo gave her his most caressing gaze. "Can you bandage hearts, madame? Mine is shattered."

"Who is it this time?" Richard said.

"Can't remember her name," he said negligently, as though already tired of the subject, but his eyes kept flashing toward Diana. "Some little actress."

She was under control now. "Frightfully sorry. Afraid I'm not a heart specialist."

"I thought you were," he murmured to her alone. *"Ecco!* I suggest a coffee, or *aperitivo.* Then we go to inspect the *macchinas."*

Downstairs, the common room was nearly full of race officials, drivers and their wives or their women, a racing reporter from *Il Messagero* in Rome and another from the magazine *La Vettura di Corsa,* with his photographer. They sat at one of the few empty tables by the bar, where Felice and Giorgio Solferino, the other two drivers of the Scuderia Barzio, were sitting.

"What will you have?" Angelo asked, his eyes moving restlessly around the room with the air of a man who is always expecting someone. "There's your friend over there."

Whether he was addressing Richard or Diana neither knew, but he was obviously referring to Hans von Lutzow, who was seated at a table in the corner, sipping some dark liquid and speaking in his sullen, superior manner to Geoffrey's chief mechanic, who stood respectfully by the table. The German looked tired.

"No friend of mine," Richard said.

"Nor mine," said Diana easily.

Angelo smiled. "I thought he was," he said apologetically.

"You're an ass at times," she said.

"Often," he said cheerfully. "It is my most engaging characteristic . . . *Bellissima!"* he said, getting to his feet.

It was Massimo's girl. She was wearing a light-blue waitress uniform and sandals, and she carried a tray.

"Buon giorno, Signor Barzio," she said shyly.

"Buon giorno, cara," he answered, his eyes flattering her; he said over his shoulder: "Forgive me, Diana. Massimo's fiancée speaks no English."

Angelo spoke rapidly in Italian, using a great many words to tell her how much more beautiful she was now than last year, although that seemed impossible to him; he told her that from now on, he, Angelo, would also consider himself engaged to her, since she had too much beauty for just one man.

Richard finally pulled his glance away from her, and found Diana watching him meditatively. "A pretty girl," he said.

"Pretty?" Diana said.

"Yes. Don't you think so?"

"No, I don't think so. She has an interesting peasant face, but I shouldn't say pretty."

Irritated, Richard said, "Neither should I. She's beautiful."

"If you care for the type," Diana said.

"I care for the type," he said shortly.

"Is she the waitress?" Diana said, her voice going high. "Because I'm perishing for something cool."

Angelo looked at her. "It is only for the fiesta. She is a very strong girl and usually she works in the olive groves tending the trees and picking the olives. She can pick more olives than most men."

"No wonder Italian women get so leathery," Diana said.

"You're charming today," Richard said.

"What will you have?" Angelo was much amused, his eyes flicking between the two women.

"Brandy," Diana said. "Not Italian. French."

Angelo ordered two cognacs, and Richard a coffee.

Ghita went toward the kitchen, and Diana said, "You were bloody irresistible just then, Dicky."

"One of my most engaging characteristics," Richard said grinning at Angelo. Diana opened her handbag and began to renew her lipstick. The two men sat silently, watching her and eavesdropping on nearby conversations.

"Ferrari coming?" Richard said.

"No.".

"That's a break." He knew Angelo did not want to discuss the race prospects in front of Diana, so he dropped the subject. It was getting hot even in the dark, musty hotel bar and Richard could feel a trickle of sweat running down the small of his back.

"How do you manage to look so cool?" he said to Diana.

She lowered the lipstick and mirror to regard him thoughtfully for a moment, before answering, "I have so little on." Her eyes widened and she added, "That's one of *my* most engaging characteristics."

Richard laughed, and she smiled demurely at them both and went back to her lipstick. The strain was broken now, and Richard felt good again, wishing they could stay this way, but not really hoping.

Ghita brought the drinks, and afterward they left Diana and walked around into the alley, taking the Solferino brothers with them. There was no particular activity in the garage because the cars had been gone over before they were trucked up to San Gregorio. After the practice session this afternoon there would be plenty of activity in the garage, but now only the coupe was getting attention, under the eye of Massimo and the chief mechanic, Pepino.

Angelo and Richard went over to them, and both men hastily wiped the oil off their hands and shook with Angelo, addressing him always as *padrone*. One of the mechanics was filing the sharp edge of the seat which had lacerated Richard's fingers; the other was pulling the wheels and brake drums. Massimo said, "It will be a bad thing if the weather is as hot on Sunday. The brakes will not last half the race. With this one, I had no brakes at all the last time around."

Angelo said, "Did you bring enough tires for this weather, Pepino?"

"I hope so, *padrone*."

"Don't hope. Be sure."

"It is not possible to estimate how fast the tires will wear until after the practice tomorrow, *padrone*."

"Why wait until tomorrow?"

"Because we will not practice today until the sun is lower and the air much cooler."

"Then we'll send a car out now, in the heat. How else can we estimate with any accuracy?"

"No," said Pepino, with anguish. "Not in this heat, *padrone*." It would hurt Pepino less to put his hand in fire.

"It is necessary," said Angelo. Whatever else might be said about him, he knew about the machines, and when he spoke this way they knew there was no use arguing. But this time Pepino did not give in.

"*Padrone*," he said reluctantly, "I do not question your

intelligence or your right to order the machines out, even if they are to be totally destroyed. But this is not fair to the machines."

"Start one up," Angelo said quietly.

"No, *padrone*," Pepino said, in agony.

"Do these machines belong to thee, or to me, Pepino?"

"Everyone knows, to thee—but they are mine, too!" Suddenly he was uncontrollably angry; he had a wrench in his hand, and now he waved it at Angelo, who did not flinch back, but stood calmly gazing at his employe. Almost in tears, Pepino went on in such a dialectic outpouring that Richard could not get very much of it. What he could understand showed a curious thread of respect for Angelo, while accusing him of being a saboteur, a rich man who destroyed things for the sake of destroying, and a sadist who was inflicting enormous cruelties on Pepino himself. Angelo listened, apparently unmoved either by Pepino's words or the tears that now streamed down his lined face. Finally the mechanic paused, sobbing for breath. Angelo said, in the same soft, intimate voice, "Start one engine."

Pepino's muscles tightened; he couldn't trust his voice, so he answered by turning and spitting on the ground.

Angelo hit him before Pepino had a chance to face him again. It was a short, hard blow, and Pepino's mouth came open and he blinked his eyes and seemed to move toward Angelo a little; and while Richard was wondering whether to intervene before the mechanic could swing the wrench, Angelo hit him again, squarely on the chin. Pepino walked limply backward three steps and then his knees went, and he fell on his back on the floor, one leg doubled under him.

There was a shocked silence in the garage. They all looked at Pepino's body lying on the dirt, then they looked at Angelo. "Put him on the cot in the corner," Angelo said calmly. The two mechanics lifted Pepino carefully and carried him over to the cot and stretched him out; he was entirely loose-jointed. Then the mechanics came slowly back to Angelo. They looked rather frightened and a little sullen.

"He does not look good, *padrone*."

"He will be all right. Let him alone."

The mechanics looked at each other, as if for reassurance.

"What is it?" Angelo said.

Giuseppe, the younger of the two, said earnestly, "You understand, *padrone,* that Pepino has been very nervous lately."

"Pepino has always been nervous."

"Yes, but it is the cancer that makes him worse, you understand. Sometimes there is much pain from the cancer."

"I know about the cancer," Angelo said.

The other mechanic stepped forward. "There is also the matter of his wife, *padrone.*"

"What about his wife?"

"She is pregnant."

Angelo looked at Richard, then back at the mechanic to say: "And?"

"But, you see, *padrone*—it was not Pepino who made the baby. His manhood has been gone for months. He said he woke up one morning and it just wasn't there any more. This is the real reason for Pepino's nervousness."

"I knew about the cancer," said Angelo, genuinely sorry, "but the matter of the wife is something else again. I will forget what has happened."

"Thank you, *padrone,*" said the elder mechanic.

"Start one engine," Angelo said.

The others relaxed from the attitudes of attentiveness they had held since Pepino was knocked down. Massimo said, "I will drive."

"Yes," said Angelo. "We might as well know the worst."

"What about the police?" Richard said.

"They will look the other way because it is the Little One."

The mechanics poured the racing fuel in the tank, while Massimo got his crash helmet and goggles out of the coupe. Then he climbed into the cockpit. The portable starting motor was wheeled into position and its shaft engaged with the end of the crankshaft. The engine started after only half a dozen revolutions, and for a long moment the garage shook from the sonic blast. Massimo closed the throttle down to a thousand r.p.m. and the noise faded to a roar over which an urgent shout could be heard.

"There's no need to kill anyone in the lower town," Angelo was saying through cupped hands, "because it's cool there anyway. So save it for the open parts of the circuit.

There's where we'll get the overheating and the tires strip-
ping treads."

Massimo nodded, watching the oil temperature gauge.

Angelo held up one hand. "Five laps only." He looked
at his watch. "Then lunch."

Massimo nodded again. The mechanics brought over the
quick-lift racing jack, which can lift the front or rear of
a racing car off the ground in one motion. They raised
the back wheels, and Massimo closed the throttle, shifted
into low gear, and cracked the throttle slightly open again,
so that the wheels were turning free, giving the back axle
and gear box a chance to warm up.

Angelo pointed to his ears and made a face, and went
out of the garage with Richard and the Solferinos following. Outside, Angelo said, "We will watch while drinking something cool."

There was not much space left in the shade under the
olive tree, but the Scuderia Barzio was much respected
among the other drivers present, and they very courteous-
ly moved their tables enough to make room for Angelo's
group.

In a few minutes the Ferrari came up out of the alley,
the engine barking rhythmically as Massimo kept blipping
the throttle. The noise racketed off the buildings facing
the piazza, until it was smothered in its own ricocheting
echoes. Massimo had apparently decided to skip the lower
town altogether, because he accelerated gently across the
piazza and went over the humpbacked bridge, and turned
sharp left off the main road onto a cart track that ran
along the ravine until it joined the road again where
it came across the bottom of the ravine from the lower
town. This way he would get two crossings of the humpbacked bridge on each lap, Richard thought, knowing the
others were thinking the same thing.

"He must be in love with that bridge," he said.

"It is a bad place," Felice Solferino said. "A very unpleasant thing."

"It is only a bridge," said his brother. "Except at speed.
Then it is the devil's nightmare."

"For the Little One," Angelo said, "a bridge is a bridge."

I am glad they feel as I do, Richard said to himself.
"He took me over it in the coupe this morning. Never
again. I get the shivers just looking at it now."

"You should know better than to go with him," Felice

said earnestly. "I do not say he will kill you, or even injure you permanently. It is what he does to you in here." He pressed his fist against his stomach.

"Old women," Angelo said. "Have a drink. It will give you courage, perhaps."

"Never mind," said Felice. "I have them, too. I'm not Pepino."

"Sunday," said Angelo. He meant it would show on Sunday whether Felice was another Pepino; he knew very well that Felice had all the necessary bravery and daring, but it was his habit to deprecate them, apparently on the assumption that it kept the Solferinos on their toes. It seemed to work with Felice, but Giorgio was another matter. In contrast to his brother's nervous alertness, Giorgio had a broad, calm face which mirrored accurately the man within. He had confidence, intelligence and a droll humor, which left no room for apprehensions.

"Sunday," said Giorgio, looking pleased. "We will have them on Sunday, too. No bigger than two peas, but we will have them, won't we, Felice?"

"Sunday," said Angelo idly. The sound of the engine thundered down at them from the amphitheater of the mountain section, and they could see it intermittently as it flashed between the trees. Everywhere around the piazza, people were watching, from tables in the sun, from windows and doorways. Two *carabinieri* appeared in the piazza, waving everyone back out of the way. The Ferrari was approaching the serpentine that led down to the bridge, and the sergeant of *carabinieri* cursed and yelled at a small boy with a donkey who was just coming out of one of the alleys; the boy looked bewildered for a moment and then his head turned toward the sound of the car on the mountainside, and suddenly understanding, he put his shoulder against the donkey's forelegs and slammed the animal over against the wall.

Out of the corner of his eye Richard saw Geoffrey, and then he saw Hans, and lastly, Diana. They had been walking from the hotel to the *trattoria,* but the noise had halted them midway. Now there was a kind of involuntary groan from the crowd, and Richard looked toward the bridge just as the machine leapt into the air. From here it did not look as though it would be back on the ground before it hit the building blocking the piazza end of the bridge, but of course it only looked foreshortened from here. Now it was on the ground, in an immense slide, and there was smoke coming from the tires and the brakes, and then a great cloud of smoke from the exhaust as the throttle opened and the revs soared to the limit. He did not hit the building, but there could not have been room for more than a shadow between them. The slide was corrected and the red car headed into the piazza, still braking hard before turning right in the square, to circle it and head back for the bridge again. Massimo used most of the open space to get around, the power coming on again at the halfway point in front of the *trattoria;* he finished the orbit in a power slide and went out of the piazza again. The crowd sighed. Richard looked for Diana.

She had not moved. Geoffrey was walking this way and Hans was about to follow him when he realized that Diana still stood with her attention fixed on the disappearing racing car. He said something to her, but she didn't seem to hear, and Hans looked off after Massimo, too, for a brief moment, and then followed Geoffrey.

"You've got something to beat," Richard said.

Geoffrey paused by the table. "A bit quick," he agreed. He went on into the *trattoria.* Hans looked at Richard as he went past, but he did not speak or show any sign of recognition. At the doorway, Hans turned and threw one more exasperated look at Diana. She was not going to move. She was waiting for Massimo, and there wasn't a power on earth that could make her move. Richard felt his stomach twisting and he stopped looking at her.

As he turned his head away, Angelo said, "I don't like it. There will be trouble, and I do not like to have trouble when it is unnecessary."

Felice, misunderstanding, said, "The tires looked all right, and he still has brakes."

"Then let Massimo use them," Angelo said, looking at Richard. "I do not want trouble."

"Don't look at me," Richard said easily.

"I am looking at you, Ricardo," Angelo said in his warm, pleasant voice. "She is here because of you."

Don't get mad at Angelo, Richard told himself, but let him keep his needle to himself. "She came with her husband," he said coldly.

"She is here because of you."

"Not any more," Richard said.

"I do not want it any other way," Angelo said.

"Then tell Massimo—don't tell me." Richard was getting angry now.

"I will tell the Little One, and I am telling you, too."

"All right," Richard said. "All right. You've told me."

"Yes," Angelo said, smiling without amusement, "I have. You won't forget, will you?"

"Skip it," Richard said in a whisper. "I don't want any more of it."

Angelo kept on looking at him with the same expression, and then he said, "I love you, Ricardo."

"Like I do you," Richard said.

"About the same," Angelo agreed, and now he was really laughing, and Richard felt the anger going. Angelo simply meant he was not blaming Richard, but that the warning still stood.

Massimo did four more laps and then crossed the piazza a final time and disappeared in the alley of the garage. The crowd in the square was breaking up, straggling off to lunch. Angelo got up, and the others rose, too, and then Diana was standing there, equally embracing Angelo and Richard with her warm smile. Neither man helped her.

"Oh, I say, you chaps, wasn't that absolutely—"

"Ripping?" asked Richard flatly.

"Oh, Dicky!" she said reproachfully; and to Angelo, "Have you asked me for lunch, caro?"

"No, cara," he said, smiling. "But I will."

Richard looked at him, surprised, but Angelo was enjoying himself.

Diana looked at her dress. "Then," she announced, "I shall change. This rag is utterly filthy." It wasn't, but no one contradicted her. Her teeth flashed in the sun, and she went off toward the hotel with long strides of her lovely brown legs.

"What the hell?" Richard said.

"You think I'm crazy? Let's go to the garage." He started off alone and after a moment Richard followed. No, I don't think you're crazy, but neither do I share your limitless confidence in yourself.

The Solferinos were already looking over the machine with Massimo and the two mechanics. Pepino was nowhere in sight.

"Where's the Old One?"

"I don't know, padrone," said Giuseppe. "We had gone to the piazza to watch the performance of this one, and when we came back, Pepino was gone from the cot."

Felice said, "He's probably cooling off with a liter of wine in the lower town."

They all knew Pepino didn't drink even wine; the condition of his insides did not permit it. But they all pretended to believe Felice.

They carefully examined the tires; heat had raised the pressure twenty pounds above normal, and in places the tread was abraded so badly there were large flat spots.

"Ten laps and you'd be on the rims," Giorgio said, "with the tread around your neck for a collar."

Angelo made a rapid calculation, then to Giuseppe he said, "Go to the hotel and phone Signor Luciano. Tell him I want forty more, and I will give him back what I don't use."

The older mechanic had finished pulling the spark plugs, and now pressed them through holes in a thin board which kept them in the proper cylinder order. He turned the board upside down so the electrodes could be seen, and they all crowded around. "Number four is oiling a little."

"And they're all too hot," Angelo said. "Use the next hardest plugs in this one this afternoon, but leave the other cars the way they are. What about the brakes?" He looked at Massimo.

"They were beginning to fade on the last lap. Not much, just a little. But I seldom touched them, you understand. I braked with the engine. If it is like this on Sunday, no one will have brakes after fifty laps."

Richard said, "And no one will have a gearbox after fifty-one."

"We will look at the linings after lunch, *padrone,* unless you—"

"After lunch," Angelo said, nodding. Then he remembered and looked at Massimo. "You are eating at the house of Ghita, Little One?"

"No," said Massimo, "she is helping Uncle Fausto, because of the crowds. So I will eat with thee, and the monster, here, and the distinguished Solferinos."

Richard put his big hand on Massimo's thin neck and squeezed a little, lifting him onto his toes. "Monster, thee said? Thou puff of unmentionable wind."

"I repent," Massimo said, forlornly. "Return me to earth."

Richard released him. "I forgive you, but you will have

to eat with the servants instead of the masters. Eh, Angelo?"

"It does not matter," said Angelo, smiling. "He is so small and insignificant we would not be aware of his presence anyway."

They went out of the garage and up the alley and turned into the hotel. Waiting for a table, they stood at the bar and had another *aperitivo,* and just as they saw Diana coming down the stairs in a fresh print dress, Giuseppe ran into the bar, his face pale. He had just found out that Pepino had packed all his personal tools and clothes, and had taken the bus down the mountain from San Gregorio ten minutes ago.

Angelo's eyes flashed with anger. "It begins."

"Was this trouble necessary, Mr. Barzio? What do we do, go after him?" Richard said.

"I could bring him back," Massimo said.

Angelo looked at Richard, indicating Massimo, and said in English, "Frank Buck, Junior. Shall we send him?"

"Unless you've got a better plan."

"It's much too simple. I have a much better plan." He answered Massimo, "Never mind; he will either come back of his own choice, or we will do without him." His eyes found Diana, who was coolly surveying the room, looking for him. "Come, we are having a beautiful lady for lunch, but do not try to eat her all at one sitting. And make sure no one else is using your plate."

Chapter Seven

FROM DIANA'S point of view, the lunch seemed a total loss. The defection of Pepino made it necessary to reorganize the pit staff. Angelo, of course, would still head the pit crew as team manager, and would direct the strategy, but there was a serious loss of mechanical knowledge in the absence of the chief mechanic. The choice of a replacement had to be made at once, assuming that Pepino would not return.

Angelo talked rapidly and easily, outlining everything. Giorgio Solferino had been a top hand with an engine before he graduated to the steering wheel; he was calm, and unlikely to spook in an emergency. He would replace Pepino, and he would be paid his regular bonus just as if he were driving. He was losing his chance of finishing in the money, but it could not be helped, and Giorgio was far too wise to complain about that. A permanent berth on a successful and solvent racing team was worth many things. After all, it was only for this one race, the last of the season.

The conversation was in Italian, and Diana could not follow it; she tried to look interested, however, and although Massimo kept looking at her when he was talking, she realized that he was only considering her with a small corner of his mind. It would have to be enough, for now.

Angelo said, "How is the hand?"

"All right," Richard said. It was sore, and he could feel the inflamed edges of the cut when he moved his fingers, but it was not throbbing, and so, probably, not infected.

"You'll drive for Giorgio," Angelo said, "if the hand is all right after practice." .

"It will be," Richard said, the dormant excitement blowing up like a balloon inside him. He had given up hope of driving again this season, so it came to him like an unopened present.

The race strategy, into which Angelo launched, would be finally decided by the weather, but there was still no indication that this unseasonable heat wave would break

53

in time. It was well known that Geoffrey's cars had engines that ran considerably cooler than the Ferraris, but they gave away pounds in radiator size and water capacity to achieve it. Geoffrey's GRP's—his machines were identified simply by his initials—would likely go all out from the start, hoping the Scuderia Barzio would accept the challenge and burn themselves out.

Angelo had no intention of doing so. He would sacrifice one machine—Felice's, because he would be carrying less overall weight than Richard—in the duel with the GRP's. Massimo and the American would hold back, at the head of the rest of the pack, saving engines and tires and brakes. The course length was slightly over two miles, with seventy laps to cover. At the halfway mark, Angelo would revise, or retain, his strategy, depending on the number and condition of the survivors.

"Understood?" he asked.

"If it is cool?" Massimo asked.

"Ricardo will set the pace. I think he can hold his own with any of the competition. If he can't, I will permit you to overtake. But I want him in front as long as possible. To save you."

Massimo looked apologetically at Richard, who said, "Never mind, Little One. I don't mind running interference. It's your race, baby."

"Ricardo—Massimo—Felice. That order," Angelo said plainly. "Until I order otherwise. Then, if possible, Massimo—Felice—Ricardo." He paused and added as if it were a small thing to ask, "I want a one-two-three-finish."

Grinning, Massimo asked, "Maybe it will rain. Uncle Fausto says so."

"Then," said Giorgio, "it will rain. About San Gregorio, Uncle Fausto tells God!"

Angelo said, "No one can touch Massimo in the wet, except sometimes Geoffrey. Von Lutzow used to be the master of all in the rain before the war, but he has lost something."

"Hitler," suggested Giorgio, and they all laughed, and then looked a little guiltily at Diana.

In English, Richard said, "A little joke about Von Lutzow's late lamented boss."

"It is very rude of us," Angelo said.

"I asked for it," Diana said cheerfully.

Massimo, making a great effort, nodded at Diana and

said to Angelo, "Say to—English lady—he are very—pretty." He blushed.

Angelo explained that a lady is a *she,* but Diana said in protest, "But that's absolutely charming, you know!" To Massimo she said quite gravely, *"Grazie mille, signore."*

"Prego." He looked pleased with himself.

For the first time since lunch had begun, Ghita appeared from the kitchen. She carried a great steaming bowl of spaghetti to the next table, and as she turned back, Angelo put out his hand, *"Cara mia,* can you take our dessert order? The boy has disappeared."

Her face was damp and the black hair shone wetly as she stood beside Diana's chair. The five men unconsciously looked at both women, and, knowing this, Diana said, "Tell Massimo she is very lovely—especially the dark skin."

Angelo nodded and repeated exactly, and Massimo smiled all over his face, but he couldn't hold it. The smile became mechanical as he looked at Diana again. Even with her rich, delicate tan you could see roses in her light skin; and for Latins, it was not enough simply to regard such skin across a table, Richard knew.

Ghita. was watching Diana meditatively. The double-edged compliment bothered her not at all, but the motive did. She looked at this elegant blonde woman and understood that she was a threat. The suppressed eagerness was plain in Massimo's face, too, and Ghita's heart turned over inside her. She did not really care what he did when he was away from San Gregorio, for that was not real. But here—that was a different matter. There was no doubt that Massimo loved her, and always would, but there was also no doubt that, given the opportunity, Massimo would take the blue-eyed woman with no more thought of the emotional damage he was causing than he would have if he were simply testing someone else's car.

"Zuppa Inglesi" would be appropriate, Di," said Richard, willing her to desist.

."It makes me ill," she said. "Since I don't have to worry about my weight, I'll have one of those chocolate meringue things. You know what I mean."

"Una Silvana," Richard said. Then in his most academic voice, he said, "Unlike Italian women, who tend to obesity by middle age, English women simply become a rag, a bone, and a hank of hair."

With a tight smile, Diana said, "You *are* a bastard, darling."

"I'm in good company," he said levelly.

"To hate so," murmured Angelo, "means to love much."

Massimo and the Solferinos had not been able to follow the words, but they sensed the general meaning. With an air almost of defiance Massimo ordered a Silvana, also. The others settled for fruit and coffee. Diana asked for a brandy. Ghita took the orders in her head toward the kitchen, and Richard was thinking, If you want to throw her away, Massimo, throw her in my direction—she's worth ten of Diana. What he said was, "You are a very lucky one, runt, and I will dance at your wedding if she is insane enough to marry you."

"Yes," said Massimo, "she will be a fine wife. Of the best. Perhaps—" perhaps after the period of lying flat on the back in the mountains—"in the spring, before the season commences again. You will be here?"

"I don't know," Richard said, looking at his bandaged hand. "I'm going home next month. After that—I haven't made any decisions."

"After the next season, maybe, when I am champion," he said eagerly, "I will come to America to see you, and I will bring Ghita, too. She has never been anywhere, you understand, and she will not be able to believe New York." He looked sheepish. "Maybe I won't believe it, either."

"If you come to see me, you'll only be halfway when you get to New York. Where I live, in California, is another five thousand kilometers."

"Is that near Hollywood?"

"Not far."

"Maybe I had better come alone."

Richard said solemnly, "You wouldn't be allowed into Hollywood without a wife."

"What?"

"The Chamber of Commerce would not give you a visa. They are trying to save the beautiful Hollywood girls for the bachelor citizens, because there are not enough of them for the foreigners, too."

"Truly?"

"Cross my heart and hope to die." That didn't make much sense in Italian, but it told Massimo it was only a joke.

"Large mound of unmentionable," Massimo said. Ghita

came back then with the meringues and the fruit, and
Massimo said to her: "Does thee wish to go with me to
New York, America?"

"If thee must go."

"Just like that, you see?" Massimo said. "She does not
believe it. There is no such place, maybe. If there is, all
right, she will go, but it does not matter either way." He
grinned happily. She gave him a look that said: *You and
you,* and left the table.

And now Angelo was describing an experimental engine
he had read about, and for which great things were expected when the formula should be changed to two-and-a-
half liters, but Richard was not paying much attention.
He was thinking about California, and he had a rush of
homesickness for it, although he realized that as soon as
he was there he would be straining to be away again. As
from a distance, he looked at the now silent blonde girl
on his right, and he wondered whether anything could ever
be the same again, and the way it was before her. It probably will, he thought, because the pattern seems to have
a habit of repeating itself. There was that other Diana
before this one, and maybe there will be another. Not if
you can help it, though, his mind said; not if you can
manage to break the pattern. It's funny how much destruc-
tion seems to be necessary before you can get at anything
worthwhile in life. And where will that kind of thinking
get you?

Diana didn't finish her brandy. She got up and left it
in her deep preoccupation with some personal mystery, and
went upstairs to her room. No one commented on her
departure; and then the lunch was over, and it had solved
nothing, really. It had started plenty of things, but that
was all.

It was siesta time, and nothing would stir for another
two hours. Richard went upstairs and along the hall, wondering, without caring, which room was Diana's. He opened
his own door and went in. It was terribly hot in the room.
The picture of the empty piazza seen through the frame of
his window shimmered with the distortion of heat waves.
He stripped to his shorts and lay down across the beds.

"Go ahead," he said aloud after a while. "Ask yourself what you're doing here. We'd like to hear the answer."

He looked straight ahead at the mottled ceiling, looking

for the answer. Several times in his life he had had the feeling that he knew it. Once, during the war, because he felt he was doing something useful. The war ended, though. The next time was in Santa Barbara, because of Marian, that other Diana—although the good part of it was before he found out she was like that; that time the answer was that she was something he needed, and it was probably not her fault that she could not sustain the image he had created out of his need. After that, nothing happened, until racing. It was simply something he wanted to do, and well. It had cost him a great deal of money— rather, he amended, it cost the Delaguardi Wine Company a great deal of money; the worry was the family's—and he had become good at it. But he would never be the best, and now he knew it. So there was no answer there any longer. Diana had never been the answer, although there had been one faint flash of hope.

So you can go back to home plate, he said. You're a lawyer, it says here on your passport. So go back to being a bright young lawyer with the nice, fat, built-in family account for number-one client. Buy Ferraris, or Pegasos, or Aston-Martins, and be a big man in the local sports-racing picture. What else can you do?

Well, he said, Angelo would keep me on if I wanted to stay. I think he would, anyway. And with luck, you wind up in a few years with some Thirds, maybe, and maybe a broken back . . . He was getting sleepy, and he turned over on his face. He thought a little about Marian, an indulgence he had not allowed himself for a long time, but it only gave him a dead feeling, so he turned her off.

He heard Massimo come out of the hotel entrance below the window, with Ghita. He knew it was Ghita by the tone of Massimo's voice, although he could not hear what was said.

Massimo's voice floated up. "No, we will not go to sleep first. We will go to sleep *after*." Pause. His quick laughter rose in the sun, and then their footsteps went away across the echoing piazza.

Grandfather Delaguardi would give me a million dollars if I brought Ghita back as my wife, Richard thought. It would be nice to have Ghita as a wife; she would be much at home with the Delaguardis, who had never really gotten over being *Piemontesi*. She would be quiet and pleasant and obedient and full of passion; and there was not a neurotic fiber in her body. He would like to have some-body like that. He went to sleep thinking that it would be fine, because he needed that kind of woman, but he couldn't think of a single thing in the world that he needed a million dollars for.

Chapter Eight

Richard awoke when someone dumped a truckload of lumber on the cobblestones of the piazza. There was not a breath of air stirring, and the humidity could not be far from a hundred per cent; he was filmed with perspiration and beneath him the heavy counterpane was soaked.

It was an effort to get up. He moved slowly and tiredly, like some huge animal coming out of hibernation. His head seemed full of wool, so that it was hard to aim his mind in any particular direction. He tried to think about taking a bath, but he had forgotten to ask where the bathroom, if any, was, and if he had to get dressed to go downstairs and ask, there was not much point to it. A china pitcher stood in a large bowl on the bureau, and it had water in it. He spread the towel on the floor and filled the bowl, and soaped himself with the unbandaged hand, and then sponged off with the spare towel. He felt a little better now, more awake, and he told himself not to drink wine in the morning any more.

He stood at the window, looking out into the piazza, while he toweled himself. It was impossible to get dry in this moist heat, but it was not important. Outside, men were erecting the long line of flimsy shelters which would serve as pits for each racing team; they stretched diagonally across the square, facing the castle and the church and a parallel line of bleachers. On the permanently lowered drawbridge of the castle, another group of men were putting up a towering booth for the judges and the electric timing apparatus. A sound truck unloaded coils of cable and nested loudspeakers on the church steps. In the path that was left between the bleachers and the pits, men with paint brushes were laying out the starting line and the grid positions for each car, but there was an argument going on.

Richard recognized the official of the racing association, who was remonstrating with one of the painters. He gestured wildly toward the bridge, and then indicated that the cars would have to come through this path at practice, and they would be running right through the wet paint.

60

The official wanted him to stop, but the painter wanted to finish painting the lines. He was gesturing now with his wet brush, and several drops apparently flew onto the suit of the official, because he backed off suddenly and pulled out a handkerchief to dab at his trousers with one hand, while speaking furiously to the painter. The man with the brush advanced again, menacingly, and now the official turned around and quickly walked away. The painter stared after him for a moment, shouting unintelligibly, and then went back to painting the lines on the cobbles.

Richard put on an old pair of cotton slacks and an open, short-sleeved shirt. It was too hot to practice in the nylon coveralls. He put on wool socks and tennis shoes, got his wallet out of his other pants, pocketed cigarettes and lighter, and started out. In the hall he realized he had forgotten his crash helmet and goggles and driving gloves, so he went back and got them out of the duffel bag. There was a dent on the helmet, and he ran his fingers over it, remembering the multiple crash at Rouen, when the car in front lost a wheel and went out of control, and Richard hit him, and another car hit Richard from behind, and all three went into the ditch at over a hundred miles an hour. Now he looked at the dent, touching it almost with respect; but he was not thinking about Rouen now, rather of the humpbacked bridge beyond the corner of the piazza. It's a good helmet, he thought, and the dent is lucky. He put the helmet under his arm and went downstairs.

Above the houses on the hillside, fantastic thunderheads were gathering in the glaring sky; it looked as though Uncle Fausto was right, and maybe the rain would break the heat spell. He looked at the house of Massimo's girl, which blindingly reflected the afternoon sun, and he thought: It must be like an oven in there, too hot for love-making; you'd feel like a baked apple. He told himself honestly that he could use that baked apple any day, and as he went around the corner and down the alley toward the garage, he wondered if he were being a schoolboy about Diana. He knew he loved her, and certainly he desired her; it was reasonably certain that it was the same way for her, but it was Richard who was holding back. He wondered if she would look at Hans, or Massimo, if Richard were her lover, and he was not thinking in terms of prowess. There would have been a bond between them that had nothing to do with—and should be stronger than—marriage. Richard's moral code was, in his opinion, simple and without hypocrisy.

They had put colder plugs in Number One, but had left the brakes and tires alone, except to reduce the pressure by five pounds; the heat of high-speed driving would quickly raise the pressure above normal anyway.

"Don't think about lap times, Ricardo," Angelo said to him. "You have seen the conditions in the piazza."

"A salad," Richard said.

"As usual," Angelo said.

"How many laps?"

"Until you have the feeling for it."

If you mean the bridge, Richard thought, I'll never have that taped; but he already had ideas about the rest of the circuit. They pushed him out of the garage, and he dropped it into low gear and then the revs came up and the whole car was suddenly alive, and he was alive with it.

At the entrance to the piazza, Richard very nearly ran into Geoffrey, in one of the G.R.P. cars; they both stood on the brakes, then both waved each other on.

"Oh—I forgot about looking up Amadeo for you," Richard said loudly over the bark of the engines.

"He found me," Geoffrey said. "Hans may be strong enough to drive after all."

"Okay," Richard said. "Go ahead."

The G.R.P. spurted across the square on a diagonal, behind the line of the pits, and Richard went after them. He took the corner by the church very slowly, because he knew the narrow streets would not be empty, despite the placards announcing the official practice hours. The Italians could be counted on for more enthusiasm toward racing, and less concern over the lethal potential of a racing car, than any other nationality.

In this section between the piazza and the open road at the lower edge of the village, there were eleven turns, and Richard no longer had Geoffrey in sight. He was simply touring now, and it was like driving in Sunday traffic. The oil temperature already showed 90 degrees Centigrade. At the last corner, he barely missed a cow, which issued nonchalantly from somone's front door, and then he was crossing the bottom of the ravine and heading up into the hollow flank of Monti di Beleri.

The engine note rose and at that exact moment he made a clean shift up into third without losing a rev; and the hot wind was beating his face. Geoffrey was in sight again, a hundred yards further up the mountain, and Richard was overtaking slowly, so he eased off a little, to hold the same distance between them. It was too early to start competing.

The road began to curve more sharply now, and over the nose of his machine, Richard saw Geoffrey start into a drift, which quickly became a slide, but was immediately controlled. Geoffrey's driving style was rather hectic, and at times looked even awkward because he was always crouched over the wheel with elbows flailing, in contrast to the great ones who sat back, holding the wheel almost at arm's length, like a farsighted man reading a newspaper. Despite the ungainliness the Englishman was a formidable opponent on the right circuits, and this was one of them. His cars had a lot of low-end torque which gave them an immense advantage on short, twisty courses, although they had to give away ten or fifteen miles an hour top speed. Well, Richard reflected, as he went precisely into a four-wheel drift around the long curve, top speed is useless on this circuit anyway. The candy belongs to the guy who gets out of the slow corners the quickest.

He knew the village lay below and to his right, and he resisted the temptation to throw a glance at it. Nor did he look at the rev counter, but peripheral vision and his own acute ear told him that the engine was peaking at close to seven thousand revolutions, and that meant he was doing better than a hundred and five miles an hour. The car was going perfectly, and there was a tight feeling of happiness that filled Richard's throat and moved out along his limbs, until his body seemed to be simply an extension of the machine itself. Sometimes, when things were right, you had this feeling, but not always; when you had it, you could do no wrong. When you had it, it was better than the greatest painter or poet or composer, and it was greater than any woman who ever lived, because it was true and perfect harmony. He found himself thinking in Italian, *Thee will need it for the bridge.*

The Ferrari came down off the concave belly of the mountain into the S-curve, in second gear now. Richard straightened out the serpentine, cutting weeds with his right wheels on the inside of the right-hand curve, and then

with his left wheels on the left-hand curve, and hè was
aimed straight down into the declivity before the bridge.
Geoffrey was already over the hump, daylight showing
under all four wheels, although much slower than Massimo had been.

Richard set himself—and suddenly the harmony was
gone. He hit the brakes and dropped harshly into bottom
gear and the tires shrieked, but it took twenty miles an
hour off his speed as he went onto the bridge. He steered
to the left, but not enough to break the wheels loose, and
for a second it looked as though the car would go right
through the railing; automatically he slammed the throttle
open and corrected to the right, and he was sliding . . .

. . . A sickening lurch into the air, followed by a neck-
cracking jolt as the car landed lopsided, and the blank
stone wall of the house rushing at him, and then somehow, through no virtue of his, they were in the clear and
heading down into the piazza. He could not remember
exactly what had happened, and he cursed himself for
doing it very badly, but at least he had not panicked. He
had known that he was not on the right line as he went
into the drift, but once he was committed, he had stayed
with it, because it was too late to do anything else, and if
he had started experimenting at the last moment, it would
have been the end.

It was necessary to drop down to a crawl as he went
through the lane before the pits, because he did not want
to get wet paint on the tires; blipping the throttle to warn
the workers out of the way, he thought the engine sounded
all right, and he hoped fervently that he had not bent
anything. He had gone into the air over the hump at full
throttle, so that the engine must have reached astronomical
revolutions, far past the permissible limit. Richard felt
very thankful that the rev counter was not the type on
which one hand remains pointing to the highest attained
number of revolutions per minute. Team managers take
a very dim view of such lead-footed carelessness.

The second lap was much better, because he approached
the bridge with full respect, taking it so conservatively
that he was able to drive straight across it without drifting,
only lifting the rear wheels clear for a fraction of a second, and making the turn beyond without strain.

Richard did eight more laps, each time with more confidence, and more speed, until he was taking the bridge

in a way he was not ashamed of. Coming into the piazza
the last time, he was about to pull over to the Scuderia
Barzio pit, where Angelo and Massimo were sitting on the
counter watching the rest of the team check over the tools
and equipment. Angelo waved him on, pointing to his
stopwatch.

It made no sense to Richard, because the streets of San
Gregorio were still not clear, but he went around again,
really trying this time, and as he turned into the S-curve,
he caught one glimpse of Angelo and Massimo standing
by the corner of the building beyond the humpback bridge.
He realized at once that Angelo was only timing him over
this section from the entry into the S, to the piazza.

Knowing this gave Richard the extra thing he needed.
He came fast through the serpentine, faster than ever before but with the machine well in hand, so that this
time he was not sickened by the thought of the bridge. He
was afraid of it still, but that was all right and perfectly
normal as long as it did not get to be the bad feeling that
told you you were on the verge of the big risk. He had
time to think that Geoffrey would refer to it as "gambling
with death." Richard grinned tightly and went onto the
bridge. The wheels came unstuck where he wanted them
to and his angle was just right as the Ferrari drifted to
the hump and was airborne; the landing was hard and
would have thrown him out of the car but for the seat
belt and the wheel, by which he held the car to him. The
power was there when he called for it and then the spinning wheels found traction again, and boosted him away
from the stone building. He headed down into the piazza
and as he passed Angelo he saw the team manager looking
at the stopwatch with Massimo craning to see it, too.

In front of their pit, Richard got slowly out of the
cramped cockpit and stretched as inconspicuously as possible. His right leg was stiff from the awkward position in
which he had to keep his foot to reach throttle and brake
because he was so tall; but he did not want to call attention to it, so he ignored the needles in his calf as the
circulation came back, and stood waiting for Angelo and
Massimo. They did not appear to be coming to the pit, and
he did not want to join them until he was sure he could
walk without limping.

The mechanics had hoisted the car on both jacks and
were changing wheels; the tires were badly shredded, with

the right rear showing fabric all the way around its circumference. Felice climbed over the pit counter in coveralls and helmet, polishing his goggles with a piece of damp chamois.

"Who else is out?" Richard said. "I didn't see anybody but Geoffrey. I only saw him the first time around."

"Adolf Hitler," Felice said. "On his first lap. With diapers."

"I have a feeling you don't like Signor von Lutzow."

"Who does?" said Felice, spitting over the car. "Even Mercedes-Benz will not have him."

Richard said nothing. The mechanics had changed all four wheels now, and they lowered the car off the jacks and Felice got in. The sun was not as strong as it had been, because the thunderheads were almost filling the sky, but it seemed even hotter. Felice looked upward.

"Soon," he said. The workmen kept looking up now, and trying to make more haste to get the canvas roofs on the pits before the rain would start. "The Frenchmen are here. With a new engine." The mechanics were waiting to give him a push-start. Felice settled his goggles. "How was it with the bridge, Ricardo?"

"It is not a bridge at all," Ricardo said, "but an invention of the devil."

"*Ecco!*" said Felice grinning. "A sincere, fornicating invention."

"*Ciao!*" said Richard. "So long."

The Ferrari rolled a few feet and then Felice let the clutch in and the engine screamed. Richard turned around and started walking toward the bridge. He remembered his hand now for the first time, and looked at the oily bandage. It was no longer neat and professional; it looked days old and he knew that the cuts had opened up and were full of oily perspiration; the fingers were stiff and the flesh felt hot under the bandage. He would have it attended to after practice finished, and perhaps Diana Nightingale would bandage it prettily again.

"Here comes the express train," Massimo said. "He looked like the Simplon Express the way he came over the bridge the last time." Angelo looked at Richard, smiling a little as he squinted in the harsh light. Massimo said, "Ricardo, thee drives more and more like Doctor Farina."

Richard was flattered, because Farina was among the

great ones, a champion who was still among the five fastest
and the three best stylists of all the European *Grand Prix*
drivers. "Not the first time over the bridge. The first time
was very poor."

"I saw," said Massimo, "from the window of the house
on the hill. Thee got started badly, that time."

"I was an old woman," Richard said.

"A cow," Massimo said. "Watching you, I said to Ghita,
look at that cow, that female elephant attempting the
bridge, and she came to the window in time to see you go
into the air like an airplane made of bricks. No, she said,
no, it is not a cow, it is a man. And I said, well, it drives
like a cow, and she said to me that I am sometimes not
very bright, and that thee, Ricardo, may be many things,
but that thee is never woman in anything."

"I kiss her hand," Richard said respectfully.

"And nothing more," said Massimo, grinning, "even
though thee is my friend."

"My friend jokes," Richard said to Angelo.

"Thy friend," Angelo said, in English. "He was thy
friend until you came over the bridge the last time. Now
you're just another bum he has to beat, so don't do him
any favors."

Angelo did not miss very much, and certainly there
was some truth in what he said, although it was ridiculous
to assume that Massimo was seriously worried about
Richard. Nevertheless, on a course like this, the margin
would not be too great, and if Massimo had any bad luck,
like a sick engine, or made one mistake, he could not hope
to make up the lost time, and Richard could beat him. But
he knew that this was not all Angelo was thinking about;
the bigger thing was that Massimo had outgrown the
Scuderia Barzio, and next season he would be in the
big leagues. Of course Angelo could take a great deal of
pride from this, because Massimo's virtuosity had developed
under Angelo's aegis, and he could always claim to
have discovered the boy and given him his chance. But
it worked both ways. Massimo had made Scuderia Barzio
the biggest single name below the level of the official
factory teams which dominated racing. Without him, Angelo was likely to have only indifferent success.

Richard looked at them both, and he thought: This is
more important for Massimo than for Angelo. He did not
know exactly why he took Massimo's side, except that he

felt like a big brother to the little Italian, whereas Angelo was simply another man whom he liked, but who was also perfectly capable of taking care of himself.

"What is being said?" Massimo asked.

"The *padrone* is afraid I will beat thee," Richard said.

"If someone must, it had better be thee, Ricardo."

They looked straight at each other, and there was no suspicion between them. The sound of a car going at full throttle through the long curve of the mountain rattled down at them and they turned to look upward to the top of the serpentine. A G.R.P. caught the sun as it turned down toward the bridge; its British Racing Green paint looked dusty and dark as the olive leaves on the hillside.

"Von Lutzow," Angelo said.

"I know."

"First lap."

"Has he driven here before?"

"No," Angelo said. "San Gregorio was never important enough for him before."

The green car slid through the serpentine and went out of sight for a moment in the declivity before the bridge. Then it seemed to explode into sight, engine roaring, tires and brakes smoking; it went into the air, slammed back down on the roadway, sliding in a dust cloud toward the building. The German corrected and accelerated out of the danger area, and turned into the piazza.

"That looked fast," Richard said.

Angelo, looking at the stopwatch, said, "A second and a half slower than you."

"My God," Richard said, appalled. He understood that it always looked worse to a spectator than to a driver, but he was not prepared to believe that Von Lutzow's frightful rush at the bridge had been any less determined than his own. "Better check it again."

"It is correct," Massimo said. "But it was his first lap. He will improve it a little."

"Did you clock Geoffrey?"

"Only his last lap. Half-second quicker than you. He may have done better before. One cylinder was dead."

Thunder rolled across the mountains from the distance, but there was no lightning yet, and no raindrops.

"Felice said the Gordinis are here," Richard said.

"If they keep running, they will be hard to beat on this circuit," Angelo said, looking at Massimo.

"Naturally," said Massimo, calmly. He was not worried.

"There's our boy," Angelo said. On the mountainside, before the entrance to the serpentine, they could see the bright red machine flashing between the olive trees.

"He has a new set of rubber," Richard volunteered.

"They were gone?"

"Real gone," Richard said. "On the strings."

Felice came down through the serpentine and over the bridge, looking very fast but not really being fast, because there was too much being wasted in unnecessary sliding and hectic overcorrecting. He cleared the building by very little. Angelo shook his head.

"He is not happy about the bridge. Not since he broke his shoulder here in forty-seven."

"What happened?"

"It was not his fault," Massimo said quickly. "He was going very well that year, was he not, *padrone?*"

"Truly."

"But the tires were not very good just after the war. He made a great jump, that Felice, and he landed very hard—perfectly, you understand, but very hard all the same. Both front tires blew right off the rims. It was very unfortunate."

"To say the least," Richard agreed politely, and added, "It's raining."

A few big drops splattered them, and there was a great flash of lightning at the mountaintop, followed almost instantly by a violent thunderclap. On signal the rain began to come down hard, and without a word, they turned and ran down into the piazza to the pit. The workmen had not finished getting the tarpaulin roof on yet, and Angelo ordered them to desist, using the canvas instead to cover the scattered tools and stacks of spare parts which lay on the cobbles.

Angelo left word for Felice to take the car back to the garage, and they ran on across the square in the rain and ducked into the hotel. Richard thought it was foolish not to practice in the rain, since there was a very good chance that it would be wet tomorrow afternoon for the race, but Angelo said, "All the water comes down off the mountain through the S-curve. It will be a river in five minutes. The lower town, too. You cannot practice for that. It is useless."

Massimo stood in the doorway, looking up at the sky.

"It will pass in an hour or two. You do not need me, *padrone?*"

They both knew what he meant. Angelo said, "Save something for tomorrow and tomorrow."

Massimo grinned. "A good well does not run dry."

He pulled up his collar and dashed out into the rain, leaping across the puddles and skidding on the greasy cobbles in his haste to be with Ghita. Already the temperature had dropped fifteen degrees. They waited by the door, grateful for the cool, wet air, and they saw the German come through the square again in the G.R.P. He was soaked, and he looked grim and intent, but this was his kind of weather and he was going around again. In a few moments Felice brought the Ferrari past the hotel and turned down into the alley; he was wet and angry, and the engine was sputtering and nearly drowned out.

Angelo left the hotel for the garage, but Richard said he wanted to change clothes, and went upstairs. He was not concerned about his wet clothes, but he was worried about his hand, and he had to carry it up in the air to keep the blood from pounding violently in his fingers.

The bandage was stuck to his palm, and the knots had tightened so that he could not untie them; it was necessary to cut it loose with his nail scissors. He tried to soak the bandage free, but gave up and peeled it away. Then he sat down very suddenly, dizzy and sick at his stomach, and waited a few minutes before looking at his fingers.

The edges of the cuts had turned white and hard, and from them, spreading toward the fingertips and deep into the palm, radiated dark streaks of red. Comparing his hands, it was easy to see that his right one was much swollen, the skin stretched tight. The throbbing was steady now, and little pains crept exploringly up his forearm.

Looking at his hand, he tried to think what to do. Perhaps the sulfa was too old and had lost its strength, or perhaps he had not used enough of it. It looked like tetanus, lockjaw. He had had it once when he was a kid, and had nearly lost this same arm, and he knew what it looked like; now he tried to remember how long it had taken to develop, but gave up because it didn't matter anyway. He sat quietly for several minutes, making a decision.

Then he opened his toilet kit and got out a new razor

blade and held a match to it; it got so hot he dropped it on the floor, and had to sterilize it again. Kicking a chair over to the washstand, he sat down and held his hand over the china basin, took a deep breath, and slashed the cuts on each of the three fingers. At the last finger his eyes wouldn't focus and he knew he was going out, and he made another desperate cut, and fainted.

He did not fall off the chair, because the washstand caught his head and shoulders, but the wounded hand hung straight down almost to the floor, and thick, dark, red drops oozed out of the cuts and dripped slowly onto the dusty boards. Richard came to quickly, and had a moment of panic at the thought that he could have bled to death. But he was alive and therefore only a fool. Feeling dazed and weak, he squeezed his wrist and palm, trying to milk more blood, but it would not run freely. His legs took him unsteadily across the room, to get the towel he had left on the bed. He wrapped it clumsily around his hand, his big body weaving. He had to get help now, because he thought he might faint again.

Can't let Angelo know, he thought; get somebody else. Where's Uncle Fausto?

Starting down the hall, he knew suddenly he was not going to make it to the stairway, and now he was not thinking clearly, and he tried to turn back to his room, but his knees wouldn't hold him, and as he fell he called out in a faint, agonized voice: "Diana—"

This time he did not completely lose consciousness, and he thought with mild irritation: This is stupid, a big hulk like you . . . Diana must have been in her room, because all at once she was there, dragging him into a room that was not his own. He could not remember what she said or what he answered, except that she did not argue with him when he kept saying that Angelo must not be told. His hand seemed to be bleeding quite nicely now, and Diana smeared vaseline on a wad of cotton and tied it onto his palm so that the cuts would not close up again entirely, but would continue to drain . . . She was gone for some time, and when she came back she had a bottle of brandy and a glass. Richard drank it thirstily, and thought his heart was going to stop; but he felt much better afterward. She said something about the Bentley and he realized she was taking him somewhere, but could he walk downstairs by himself without attracting attention?

He didn't know, but he said flatly, "Yes."

She helped him up and he leaned on her as far as the head of the stairs. She went down first, casually, and Richard followed, holding the railing with his good hand, but there seemed to be little strength in it. He could not have said whether there were any witnesses in the bar, because he looked straight ahead at the back of Diana's golden head, and then they were outside.

The black Bentley was waiting in the rain. Diana opened the door for him and he got in slowly, and at that moment Hans von Lutzow came running along the side of the piazza, head ducked down against the rain. He saw Diana and came over to her, saying something imperative. She did not bother to answer but started around the front of the car, and the German put his hand on her arm to detain her. Her face stiffened and she said something in a low, frozen voice and he pulled his hand back and stood there staring at her, the water dripping off his white face, as she got into the car and drove out of the square. Richard had watched, but none of it seemed real, and he no longer had any curiosity about it. As soon as they turned the corner by the castle moat, he leaned forward and put his forehead on his knees, because he did not want to lose himself again.

Chapter Nine

〔 I Principe Vittorio Sacriponti sat in a raffia chair on the shaded end of the castle terrace overlooking the valley and the glittering segment of sea far below. He was a slender, elegant man of sixty who contrived, with the unlimited means at his disposal, to pass for forty. Angelo, who knew him well, patronized the same tailor and shirtmaker, masseur and coiffeur; he had not been able to learn the identity of the prince's corsetmaker.

"It is not only not wise, it is most irritating," said the prince. "But it was simply impossible to get the staff here from Cannes a day earlier. Those fools made such a bother at the frontier because Piero had a small quantity of morphine in his pocket."

Angelo put down his cigar and took a sip of his Scotch and soda. "A pity," he said, not caring at all about the majordomo's trouble at customs.

"And, of course, the idiots detained the whole staff overnight, and now there isn't time to prepare things properly, so I have had to postpone the dinner until tomorrow night. I dislike the position intensely," he said in anguish. "You must understand that, Angelo."

"A pity," Angelo said again.

"It's quite sickening that my entire schedule be torn to shreds this way. To give the dinner party the night before the race! It makes me a fool before the fiesta committee, and for what? A miserable few grams of morphine! It could not have happened in the old days. These republicans!"

Angelo was not listening, because he was more concerned about the possible jeopardy of his own plans. He did not approve of his drivers eating and drinking heavily the night before the race, and he knew it was nearly impossible to avoid excess at the prince's parties. It was a further annoyance that he would have to postpone his curiosity about Diana for another twenty-four hours—so many rooms in the castle, so easy to become conveniently lost from the others—and that made him start worrying about Richard again. The black Bentley had gone down the mountain two hours ago; in Angelo's experience, if one went off with a married woman, one did not hasten to return.

"Do you want some smoked salmon?"

Angelo looked up. The prince was regarding him with impatience over a tray of antipasto held between them by the culpable majordomo.

"Sorry," Angelo said. "A little, thank you. And the gray caviar."

The prince served him, adding peppers and artichoke hearts soaked in oil, and anchovies.

Then for a few minutes they ate in silence, Angelo's glance straying to the dusty white ribbon of road down the valley to the darkening sea. From the village side of the castle came the sound of a band, and occasional firecrackers.

"It begins," said the prince, and Angelo nodded, but they made no move to cross the terrace and look down on the piazza.

Out of duty, Angelo said, "It is a fine thing that you do this for the village, Vittorio. It brings much extra money each year."

The prince waved a forkful of salmon. "Yes," he said comfortably, "one has, naturally, obligations to one's people, and this is one of the least unpleasant ways of discharging them. Thus, everyone is satisfied for another year."

The sun was gone now, and the air was dry and almost cool after the storm. The noise ballooned above the piazza, borne upward on a solid current of smells, of onions and frying fish.

With distaste, the prince said, "If the wind doesn't change, we shall have to go inside."

"I don't mind it," Angelo said, adding maliciously, "most of us have some peasant blood somewhere along the line."

"I daresay," the prince said politely and without belief. "But I seem to have lost my appetite for the moment."

So had Angelo, for he had just become aware of a car winding up the road from the coast; it was the Bentley.

"What pleases you?" demanded the prince.

"Your excellent caviar," Angelo said, letting the light go out of his eyes.

"I know better," Vittorio said with interest. "You may be a gourmet, but your tastes are not confined to food. There is a lady, Angelo?"

Angelo gave him a long stare, then all at once he laughed, his white teeth of an unreal brightness in his dark face.

"But, naturally!" he said "Naturally, one hopes. She is an English milady, very peculiar."

"Do I know her?"

"The Countess of Partingbridge. Very blonde. Very—English."

"And the earl?"

"Here, also. A great racing enthusiast. Even more peculiar than his wife. He permits himself to be cuckolded regularly."

"With you, my dear Angelo?"

"Who can tell? There is much competition."

"From?"

"There is a young American driving for me this year. Quite rich, I think, and quite impressive. He is as big as the two of us."

"Ah," said Vittorio. "He works for you. You can control him."

"Perhaps, perhaps not. He is in love with her, I think. It is very hard to tell with Americans and English." He added, "There is also Von Lutzow, who apparently was permitted the boudoir once, and now considers it his right. And finally—" frowning—"there is Massimo."

Vittorio sat upright. "Massimo!"

Angelo nodded. "Even he is sniffing around, although I do not underestimate Ghita's hold on him." At the prince's lack of comprehension, Angelo said, "Ghita—Margherita Pilbo. She lives right over there—Massimo's fiancée." He waved toward the houses on the hill, but the prince was not interested in discussing a peasant girl.

"I wish to meet this Englishwoman, Angelo."

One more dog catches the scent, Angelo thought with amusement. "Don't worry; the race committee's sure to include her in your invitation list."

"I prefer to extend this invitation personally." He stood up. "I have changed my mind—it's only proper that I appear at the fiesta the first night." They were walking toward the parapet overlooking the piazza, and now over the cacophony of the villagers, Angelo heard the muted,

velvety roar of the Bentley coming up the last sharp climbing turn past the castle moat.

"She is here?" the prince said. "And available?"

The Bentley halted before the hotel and Angelo watched
Diana get out of the driver's seat and wait until Richard
came around from the opposite side of the car, and then
they went into the hotel without touching.

"She is here," said Angelo, "but I cannot promise you
that she is available."

The hotel bar was so full of people that Angelo and
the prince made very slow progress; everyone wished to
greet His Highness personally, everyone wished to buy a
drink for the true *padrone* of San Gregorio. "This is very
undignified," Vittorio said to Angelo, "I should not have
come here."

"It's too late now," Angelo said, unfeelingly, "and anyway, it makes a very impressive entrance."

All eyes followed their progress to the table where
Richard and Diana sat with Geoffrey and Von Lutzow;
Angelo performed the introductions against a rather sudden background of silence. The prince was at his most
elegant and charming; his nobility was impeccable; without the slightest suggestion of condescension, they were
all still aware that Vittorio was the host and that he
was favoring them above all others. Geoffrey was, perhaps, the one exception; he was eminently preoccupied
with the braised oxjoint. When Vittorio bowed to him and
said, "My lord," Geoffrey put down his fork, wiped his
hand, offered it and said, all in one word, "Howjado?"

Another small table was added, despite Vittorio's protest against disturbing their meal—no, he regretted being
unable to dine with them, but his doctor had placed him
on a severe regime, of which only his personal chef had the
formula. But he would take a glass of wine with them,
gladly.

They were speaking in English during these prelimi-
naries, so that Angelo was able to say to Richard in
Italian, "Thee appears to be a bit pale, my friend."

Richard was keeping the bandaged hand out of sight on
his lap, and it was a moment before he understood that
this was Angelo's way of asking if an amorous interlude
had just passed. It was better so, because he did not want
any questions about the real purpose of the trip down the

mountain, and Angelo's one-track mind apparently har-
bored no suspicions.

"In this heat," Richard said blandly, "one can overtire
too easily."

"The admission of weakness is the beginning of wis-
dom," Angelo said, smiling. Vittorio heard him and said
in English, "Angelo is being profound; it's the quality of
his which I least admire, since I totally lack it myself."

Diana said, "This is getting frightfully intellectual. Say
something, Dicky. Show them you went to college."

Richard grinned tightly. "You think the rain will hurt
the rhubarb?"

Geoffrey looked at him and his mouth twitched. "Jolly
good, old boy. Serves her right."

"Don't pretend you know what it means," Diana said to
him.

"Know it's profound, though," Geoffrey said with satisfaction, and dropped out of the conversation.

Vittorio was not pleased, having completely lost the reins.
He stood up, took Diana's hand and kissed it; his attitude remained above reproach, but he managed to convey
the idea that this was not a farewell, rather a promise for
the future. "My house is at its best when there is a great
beauty within its walls. Tomorrow night my house will re-
live the glories of the past because you will be there,
madame."

He bowed once more and left them.

"Never saw it done better at the Old Vic," Diana said.
"Is he real?"

"No," said Angelo. "We simply blow him up with a
tire pump once a year for the race."

"Fancies himself, rather, I should say."

"Women seem to find him charming," Angelo said.

"Oh, I think he's lovely," Diana said, "but you know, I
kept thinking he'd forgotten his plumed hat and sword."

"Not that old," Geoffrey said.

"Don't talk so much, darling," Diana said gently.

The band in the square was playing something which
sounded like a fascist marching song, but in the hotel bar
no one paid any attention. Richard and Diana were not
hungry because they had stopped at a café on the shore
after leaving the clinic, and he had eaten a large steak,
almost raw, and drunk a liter of Chianti, on the doctor's
orders. He was very tired now and weak, and he wanted

to go to bed, but it would be necessary to stick it out as long as Angelo was around.

The dinner seemed interminable, because Angelo did not miss a single course. Richard and Diana only picked at their food, while the silent Von Lutzow ate remorselessly, his sullen eyes moving from Diana to the American and back again.

"Do hurry up, Geoffrey," she said again. "I want to go to the fiesta."

"Forgive me, will you?" he answered; knowing she would. "Spot of work to do tonight."

"I will take you," Von Lutzow said.

"For the fiesta, you should be escorted by a native," Angelo said. "I offer myself."

"We'll all go," Richard said. *"The Scuderia Diana."*

"Ripping," said Geoffrey, and they left the table.

The piazza was brilliant with multicolored paper lanterns, and almost solid with temporary trestle and canvas booths for the purveying of wine and coffee, ice creams, all varieties of *pasta* stuffed with fish and meat and cooked in the ubiquitous olive oil. There was no formal dancing platform, any clear space on the cobbles sufficing. A crowd of villagers before the booth of the wheel of fortune suddenly broke into a dance, the men rakishly clutching their private wine bottles; there was no rigid pattern to the dances, for most of them were attempting the steps of the peasant dances centuries old, while some of the young men, who had been further afield, were doing a rather frenzied, free-style jitterbug, with so much shouting from the boys and squealing from the girls that the band could scarcely be heard.

The village was still divided, for the fiesta was too young to have absorbed the outsiders, who moved about the piazza in rather self-conscious groups.

"I feel as if we were butting in," Diana said.

"There is a cure for that," Angelo said. He went to the nearest wine booth and bought four large *fiascos*, the straw-covered bottles of Chianti. Rather solemnly they waited while Angelo uncorked and handed a bottle to each.

"To the fiesta," Angelo said, and took a long drink.

What a day this has been, Richard thought, drinking lightly; and it doesn't seem to be over yet. "All right," he said, "what do we do now?"

"You wish to dance?" Angelo said to Diana.

"I'm not cured yet," she said.

"Then," said Angelo, "we will be tourists, for the moment." No one else was allowed to spend money. Angelo bought them all funny paper hats and noise makers and paper streamers and confetti, and for Diana a beautiful lace shawl which she wore over her head like the native women. Automatically they kept drinking from the *fiascos* and suddenly without realizing it they had passed the meridian and crossed over into a new country of slightly hazy romanticism, and they belonged to the fiesta.

Richard said cheerfully, "This is at least the second time I've been drunk today." He was even prepared to be charitable toward Von Lutzow, whose dogged silence they were all trying to ignore. The German was drunker than any of the other three, but the only change the wine had made in him was an abandonment of his former sullen moroseness; now he carried himself with an attitude of excessive superiority, seeming to hold himself aloof from the childish proceedings of the inferior races, while still managing to hover at Diana's elbow in the role of protector.

Later, they sat at the tables beneath the olive tree, and watched Diana dance with one of the village boys; she did steps she had never heard of, and did them well, and then, the boy becoming emboldened, they were jitterbugging wildly.

"A woman of great fantasy," Angelo said.

"A fantastic woman," Richard said more accurately. He felt no jealousy, and no desire; for the moment he was relaxed and at peace. Once or twice he had forgotten about his bandaged hand and allowed it to come into view, so that Angelo had noticed the fresh bandage, and had seemed on the verge of commenting. When this happened Richard made a great show of using that hand to hold the heavy *fiasco* while he drank, and Angelo simply looked and said nothing. The doctor at the clinic had been very thorough, and there was now a tiny drain tube fixed into a new incision in the palm of his hand. He did not feel any real pain, but the hand seemed very heavy and the fingers were clumsy and stiff.

Suddenly Angelo said in a startled voice, "There's Pugliero! Over there at the ice cream stand—"

"Does that mean the Maseratis will be here after all?"

"It wouldn't surprise me," Angelo said grimly. "They're crazy not to come, when it must look like a fairly easy win for them." He was not enjoying the fiesta now, and he looked around the piazza broodingly. "I wonder where Massimo is. Have either of you seen him this evening?"

Von Lutzow shook his head faintly. Richard said, "Must be somewhere with Ghita. I haven't seen her around, either."

The music stopped just then and all the faces in the square turned toward the church. A huge man had just come out onto the steps, and it was a moment before Richard recognized Uncle Fausto, because he was wearing a frock coat and the tricolored sash of office as the mayor of San Gregorio. Followed by two other dressed-up villagers, he made his way at a stately pace across the square, the crowd falling back respectfully, to the stand which had been erected at the castle gate for the racing judges. When he had mounted the stand and faced the crowd, the band began to play again.

"What goes on?" Richard said.

"It must be *La Regina di Fiesta*. I thought it was postponed until tomorrow night."

Diana hurried back to the table, flushed and excited.

"I'm dying of thirst," she said. "Too cold for that sort of thing, you know. Where's my private stock?" Richard pushed a bottle across the table to her. "Are there going to be speeches?"

"I'm a stranger here myself," Richard said.

At this moment a procession of young girls, all in white, and each carrying a long lighted candle, filed slowly from the church and down into the square. The priest remained standing in the doorway, smiling after them.

"What *is* it?" Diana demanded.

"There she is," Richard said. "There's Ghita."

"It is the ceremony of the Queen of the Fiesta," Angelo said. "It is a very old tradition, long before there was any race. All the young virgins of the village—who have just turned seventeen this year—compete for the title of queen. It is a very great honor to be chosen. The queen is invited to the dinner at the castle, and she spends the night in the royal tower suite, with everybody, including Prince Vittorio, waiting on her."

"I'll bet that old goat waits on her," Richard said.

"Don't be dirty. I think it's charming," Diana said.

"Well, I wouldn't let any seventeen-year-old virgin of mine sleep in that castle," Richard said.

"That designation is itself an anomaly," Angelo said. "Don Ludovico clearly must forget everything he has heard in the confessional before blessing the eleven young virgins of San Gregorio."

"You're all disgusting," Diana said. "Let's do go over there and watch." She jumped up without waiting and started toward the judges' stand in the wake of the crowd flowing behind the procession of young girls.

"Seventeen's a little old for you, isn't it, Angelo?" Richard said, when the other man got up with alacrity.

"I am only seventeen myself," said Angelo. "Tonight, that is."

They ran into Massimo at once, in the crowd milling around the base of the judges' stand. His eyes were enormous with excitement as he seized Angelo and Richard by the arms and propelled them into the very forefront of the audience.

"See her? There she is, right there? See her? Isn't she beautiful? Tell me, isn't she? Do you think she will win? How could they choose anyone else?"

There was a low stage in front of the judges' stand where the girls now took their positions overlooking the crowd in the piazza. Most of them were carefully demure, but there was one girl who could not stand still. She was beautiful in the most obvious fashion; the soft, plump curves of her body and the provocative eyes and mouth were making a powerful effort toward the crowd, and they were not insensitive to her. It was obvious that she was the only serious competition to Ghita, who waited quietly with her almost awesome dignity, her face full of love as her eyes never left Massimo.

"She must be chosen," Massimo said feverishly. "She didn't want to do it, but I said she must, for me."

Richard looked at Massimo for a moment, then his eyes met Diana's, but she was wearing the blank, defensive expression again, and he turned once more to Ghita.

Uncle Fausto waved his arm and the band dribbled off into silence. He cleared his throat, rubbed his nose with the back of his huge hand and spoke in his great voice that boomed and echoed across the piazza: "Citizens of San Gregorio, honored and esteemed guests . . ."

Richard let the words pass across the surface of his

brain without registering. I am drunk, he said to himself, much drunker than I had realized. I must be very drunk, and if I had any sense at all I would go back to the hotel and knock myself out with a couple of sleeping pills— because I am in love with Ghita. When he heard that inside his mind he felt frantic for a moment and he stumbled a little against Angelo and said out loud, "That's ridiculous . . ."

The speech was finished and now Uncle Fausto began introducing the girls. "Signorina Luciana Maria Aida Paoli!" There was indiscriminate applause from the crowd, for Uncle Fausto had wisely started with the least attractive girls.

"Signorina Anna-Maria DiBlazio—"

"Signoria Josephina Margherita—"

"Signorina Isabella—" The seductress. As the audience boomed its authentic applause, she wooed with face and body and the *vivas* went up another notch.

"Signorina Margherita-Luisa-Theresa Pilbo!"

"Hurray!" roared Richard. *"Viva, viva!"* This I give you, Ghita, my breath and my voice, because it is all you wish from me. He was suddenly conscious that his voice dominated all others and he threw a glance toward Massimo; but Massimo was not standing in his former place. He was electioneering. Moving through the crowd like a dervish, he was yelling and pointing at Ghita and wherever he went the applause rose even higher, for the crowd was being reminded that Ghita was the chosen of Massimo, the hero of the village. At last the noise died of its own weight.

In the following silence Richard found Diana staring at him. Her mouth was slightly open in pained surprise, and his heart twisted a little, sensing that she had understood. In the next moment she was gone through the throng. Good-bye, he said, and how many good-byes do you need before you get one that takes?

Uncle Fausto and the other judges were in conference on the platform, apparently deciding on the basis of the applause. Richard said anxiously, "There isn't any doubt, is there?"

"It is very close," Angelo said absently, looking off after Diana.

The crowd waited, in a torment. Uncle Fausto shook hands with his colleagues, then lighted another candle and came down to the level where the girls waited. He walked directly to Ghita and put the second candle in her hands. Her rival turned pale and looked as though she might faint for a moment, and the other girls were close to tears. The audience yelled its approval, as Uncle Fausto said something which seemed to cheer the runner-up, Isabella, who went eagerly onto the judges' stand and came back with a small golden crown, which she placed on Ghita's bowed head. For Isabella would be lady-in-waiting, and it was something to set her above the other girls, although she had not been chosen queen.

"She gets to come to the party, where I may be able to console her." But Angelo's heart was not in it. Von Lutzow had disappeared too.

Richard let his voice run down. He stood watching as Ghita readjusted her crown, and for a moment their glances met, and she smiled—it seemed to him—apologetically, as if to say: it is all very childish, as you can see, but then, it is pleasing to Massimo.

Again the band was playing and Ghita came down from the platform and danced a formal measure with Uncle Fausto, and then with the two judges, and then with Massimo. Richard sat on the edge of the platform and drank the rest of the Chianti, waiting for his turn. Angelo was already consoling Isabella, who had fully recovered her composure and was aggressively bewitching him.

Massimo beckoned then, and Richard stood up and went across the cobbles to them.

"The queen wishes to dance with thee, monster." Massimo was bursting with pride. "Be careful thee does not crush her."

Again the quiet, warm smile, and she was in Richard's arms, as light, as graceful as he had known she would be, and he was ashamed because of his fatigue and the wine.

"I am embarrassed," he said. "I am not worthy of this honor." He thought he was teasing, but even to his ears the words sounded unexpectedly sincere.

"The honor is mine, Signor Delaguardi."

"It would please me to be called Ricardo by Your Majesty."

"And we," she said with complete naturalness, "should be pleased with less formality, Ricardo."

"Thank you," he said humbly. "But I say this in all

honesty, not meaning it as a joke: I have never known anyone more worthy of the title." He stumbled a little on a loose cobble, and added: "Clumsy as I am—drunk as I am—I offer myself as your true knight and devoted servant."

She was tall enough so that, of all the men in the village, she had to look up only to Richard and Uncle Fausto. Now, as they danced in silence, her wide dark eyes were raised thoughtfully to Richard's face.

"What makes thee unhappy, Ricardo?" It was the first time she had used the intimate form with him.

"I am happy."

Quickly she said, "I was wrong to speak of it."

"No," he said. "It was kind of you to be concerned."

Following the thought, she said, "She is very beautiful, Ricardo. I have never seen anyone like her before, so—white, so rose, like china. She is very beautiful, but I do not think she is very happy, either."

"That may be very true," he said.

"Perhaps," she said after a moment, "it is not enough to be rich, and noble."

"No. Although it is a matter of definition."

"*Definizione?*" she asked. "I am very ignorant, Ricardo."

"It is the meaning of words. She is rich, and noble—it is not enough. You, also, in—"

"Thee keeps saying 'you.' "

"Out of respect, not unfriendliness; I will remember." He went on quickly, "Thee, too, in another sense of the words, is rich and noble—and it is enough. Thee is happy." He finished almost accusingly.

"I wish that thee could be, too."

"It isn't important," Richard said roughly. He wanted to get away right now, but the villagers were shy about interrupting while she danced with a foreign guest, and he could not call on either Massimo or Angelo, who were occupied with other partners. He did not want to say anything foolish that might lower him in Ghita's esteem—he was aware that she admired his size and strength, academically, as one might appreciate the heroic proportions of a statue; and he suspected that she even matched him, subconsciously, against herself. "Do you want something to drink?" he said in desperation.

"As thee wishes," Ghita said, to please him.

It was easier now that he was not touching her, and they stood by the booth of the ice creams and fruit drinks, and they both had lemonades, and she said, "Thee longs for home?"

That was the toughest question of all, and he did not know how to answer. Everything seemed unfinished and unfulfilled, at home and abroad, and he had the honesty to admit that it was only the reflection of the emptiness he dragged everywhere with him.

"No," he said finally, "places are not enough, either."

"Thee badly needs love, Ricardo."

"Yes." His voice was stifled. Don't ask her what she means—she means exactly what she says, but—was there something behind it? You utter fool, he said to himself sarcastically. . . .

He had never known anyone with her direct simplicity, apart from his grandparents, with whom she had so much in common. Away from home he had grown up in a society where the devious was the norm, in a world of unfinished sentences, abandoned in midair—for nothing must be what it seems, and is only a disguise for some dark and threatening complexity hiding in the shadows of the mind.

Ghita saw his emptiness and his need, that was all. She was not offering herself; she was offering friendship, and if he did not wish to lose it, he had better not make the mistake of assuming double meanings . . . But far back in his mind he knew persistently that there would not always be Massimo; he slammed the door on the thought. . . .

"I need sleep more," he said easily. "Until tomorrow, Ghita."

The wide eyes did not leave his face. "Sleep well, Ricardo."

"*Ciao*," he said, and went away from her through the noisy crowd.

A learned English journalist of the motoring press was standing drinks in the bar; he was extremely drunk, and tottering slightly beneath the weight of his massive dignity, as he quoted from a lecture he had heard on how to determine race results in advance, by the cunning use of a slide rule and the factors of power, weight and frontal area; the formula was nearly always right, theoretically—it was the unexpected and incalculable factors, like the burst tire, dirt in the fuel, metal fatigue or the omnipresent human error, that contradicted it.

"Have a drink, Yank," the journalist called, waving his glass at Richard and getting half the contents on his already sodden vest.

"Gotta see a friend," Richard said. He went past into the back corner of the bar, because Geoffrey was there, and at the moment, Diana's husband was his creditor.

There was a half-eaten sandwich and an empty milk glass on the small table, and Geoffrey was asleep with his head leaning back in the corner. He wasn't very clean; only a small portion of his face, around the actual features, was clear of oil, as if he had washed while looking in a too-small mirror. He looked very tired.

Richard sat down. "Geoffrey."

Without opening his eyes, Geoffrey said, "Hello."

"Why don't you go to bed?"

After a while Geoffrey opened his eyes. "Might do."

"That's good, old bean," Richard said.

With interest, Geoffrey said, "Bit squiffy, what?"

"Quite," Richard said. "Fractured. I'll buy you one."

"Don't mind."

"That's our Geoffrey," Richard said. "Eager! Enthusiastic! Ebullient!" He checked himself from pounding on the table. He didn't know what impelled him, but he had an almost irresistible urge to behave the way Americans in Europe do. He said heavily to Geoffrey, "I *am* American, you understand."

"That's all right, old boy," the Englishman said.

"Thanks very much." Suddenly he bellowed across the bar: "Strega! *Subito, subito!*" Everybody looked around, so Richard stood up and bowed. The journalist bowed back, and they all laughed. Richard sat down with exaggerated heaviness and said to Geoffrey, "American, by God."

"Oh, quite."

"Entirely," Richard said, with emphasis. He was feeling dejected now because of his growing embarrassment with Diana's husband, and he wanted the drink right away. He banged his fist on the table. Geoffrey caught the milk glass but the remains of the sandwich danced off the plate and landed in Richard's lap.

Richard held it up suspiciously. "This yours?"

The other said absently, "Go right ahead."

"Thanks very much." Richard didn't want it and didn't think he could swallow it, but he couldn't stop himself. He ate the whole thing in three bites, and then the bottle of Strega was on the table. "Sometimes," he said, "I behave even worse than this." He was filling the little glasses. "Stick around. It will horrify you."

"Here's to the horrors," Geoffrey said.

"Never met one I didn't like," Richard said.

"What?"

Richard didn't hear him. He said suddenly, "I'm going home."

"Haven't tasted your drink, you know."

"I don't mean upstairs, damn it. Home. America. The U.S.A. The-good-ole-U.S.A.-unquote."

"Well, cheer-o," Geoffrey said. "Better drink up first."

"Not this minute," Richard said patiently. "After the race. Right after the race." He swallowed the Strega without tasting it. "Right after the last great big nothing of my racing career. Did you get that?"

"Not half. Does it matter?"

"No." He looked at Geoffrey and spoke very distinctly. "The short, nothing-romance of Richard Delgard."

After a time, Geoffrey said, "Out of the lists, eh?"

"Unhorsed. Kindly do not say 'Rotten luck, old bean.' " Geoffrey's mouth twitched once, but he said nothing.

"That rot I was talking this morning—forget it."

"Rather."

"I'm sorry."

"Don't go on about it, old bean."

"I won't, old bean." There was nothing more he had to say now, not on any subject, although he tried to find something because he still felt vaguely that he hadn't wiped out his debt to Diana's husband. After a while he thought of something.

"Thanks for the drink," Richard said, and went out of the bar and up the stairs, thinking: That's one thing I don't mind owing him for.

Chapter Ten

On Saturday morning the piazza looked like a battleground. Richard counted twelve bodies in plain view of his hotel window; and how many others lay hidden in the pit shelters and the carnival booths was hard to imagine. They slept as they had fallen, tranquil in the morning sun. The square was a litter of raffia-sheathed wine bottles, crepe-paper streamers, ice cream wrappers, paper cups and plates and all the other grimy confetti of carnival morning-after.

Richard had coffee and a sweet roll under the olive tree, but he refused the wine of Signor Guerrerra. "I had too much last night, and there is serious practicing to do today."

"It will be even crazier tonight," said the proprietor. "As a citizen, I deplore it; but as a businessman—well, it is very good business."

Although it was now after eight o'clock, Richard was still the only foreigner abroad in the village. Even the natives were scarce—this morning, the parade to the fountain brought out only the very old and the very young.

It would be hot again today, he decided, but not the way it had been yesterday. Despite the amount and variety of alcoholic beverages he had consumed, he felt fine, except for the hand, and even that seemed less painful as long as he didn't flex the fingers. He went around into the alley to see if there was any activity in the garage.

Giuseppe and Tullio were still lying on their cots in their best clothes, which were rumpled and stained; the smell of wine dominated the familiar odors of mustiness, of racing fuel and grease and oily metal. They were smoking contentedly while they waited for coffee to boil on the portable alcohol stove. They both said, *"Buon giorno, signore,"* but only the elder mechanic, Giuseppe, stood up. He was a little unsteady, and it shamed him before Richard. But the younger one said familiarly, "Some night, eh? How many girls you get?"

"I got only drunk, Tullio."

"Should have come in here," Tullio said happily. "It was like a harem, I tell you—" He stopped talking because Giuseppe said something to him in a sharp undertone.

"He talks like a man still drunk," Giuseppe said to Richard. "I wouldn't allow any strangers in here, *signore.*"

"I wasn't even listening," Richard said. He went out through the alley, passed the church, and went up the narrow, worn stone stairway that led to Ghita's house. It was very steep and both his heart and his hand were pounding when he reached the level of her doorway. He knocked softly, using his left hand.

"Massimo?" he said. "It's Ricardo."

"Let him enter," he heard Massimo say inside.

"No," Richard said to the closed door, "I don't want to disturb you. I only want to borrow your car to go down to the clinic."

"Let him enter!" Massimo's voice was urgent. Then, Ghita's soft, warm voice came in answer. "Patience— would you have me go to the door in my skin?"

"No," said Massimo. "He is very old-fashioned, and would certainly fall dead of shame." This was said loudly to be sure Richard would hear, and the latter had a moment to look at Ghita, thus, in his imagination, before she opened the door.

She was wearing an unbelievably garish Chinese kimono —obviously a gift from Massimo—and her black hair fell loose below her waist.

"Buon giorno, Ricardo."

He stammered something formal to her and they shook hands, and he found himself drawn into the room. Massimo sat propped up in bed, drinking coffee. He was naked to the waist, and Richard involuntarily looked at the pathetic chest, and wished he had not.

"Prepare breakfast for my friend," Massimo ordered. "Sit down, monster, and tell me the news."

"Please—no breakfast. I've already eaten." He was sorry he had come up here, because he did not like thinking about Ghita in this connection; it bothered him even to meet her eyes.

"Sit down," Massimo said again, so he sat by the table, and Ghita poured out a cup of coffee and then placed a basket of oranges and bananas before him. He realized that it would be insulting to persist in refusing hospitality, so he said, "It's very kind of you. I apologize for disturbing you so early." He peeled a banana.

"We are honored," Ghita said. She would not go back to the bed as long as was here, Richard knew, nor did Massimo seem to expect her to. She simply stood back a little, out of the line of vision, respectfully, so the men could talk.

"The coffee is excellent," Richard said to the room, "and the banana is exactly ripe."

"Never mind all that," Massimo said. "How goes the hand?"

"It is fine," Richard said, hoping it was true. "I only want the bandage changed before practice."

"I am very sorry about that," Massimo said. "It must be very painful."

"It is not important. You don't mind if I take the car?"

"You're welcome to it. Or, perhaps," he added, too solicitously, "it would be better for me to drive, if the hand is sore?"

"No, thanks," Richard said emphatically.

Massimo giggled like a child. To Ghita he said, "The monster thinks it is unsafe to ride with me."

She smiled at Richard. "Ricardo is as sensible as he is big."

"And I am a midget—and therefore an imbecile?" Massimo demanded. "I will have to beat this woman more often."

"Need anything from town?"

"A whip. A large whip."

"Anything else?" he asked from the door.

"A chain. For when the whip breaks."

"Whips and chains," Richard said, as if memorizing. "How about a nice rack, or a thumb-screw?"

"That's the idea," Massimo agreed. "The latest model, with plenty of chrome."

"What a lot of nonsense men talk," Ghita said, going toward the bed. "Cover up the chest, foolish one. It would be very undignified for a great champion to die of a cold."

"Thanks for breakfast," Richard said. "And don't worry about the car— I drive intelligently." He went out, but Massimo yelled after him:

"Be careful how thee gets into the car, monster, that it doesn't split at the seams, like trying to wear the pants of thy little brother!"

The Ferrari went down the mountain in third gear so that it would not be necessary to shift for acceleration out of the hairpin turns. He drove fast, using his left hand only, and it was very pleasant to be at the wheel, even though the custom body had been tailored for a man half his size.

The seaside resort town was overrun with Saturday shoppers, but he found a parking place on the shady side of the main street and walked back to the clinic.

Doctor Alciade did not keep him waiting. He came into the waiting room, dazzling in red slacks and white jacket of raw silk, and a smile of matching brilliance. He obviously expected Diana, so Richard said, "Afraid I'm alone, doctor."

The young doctor sagged into such utter disappointment that Richard would not have been surprised to see him weep. So he said pointedly, "Didn't dare knock on her door at this hour of the morning. There's a limit to what one asks of casual friends."

Incredulous, Doctor Alciade said, "But I thought—" and let it hang in the air.

"You thought wrong," Richard said, thinking, No wonder he's confused—I can hardly keep up with this myself.

Immensely relieved, the doctor was able to reassume his professional bearing. His hands were adept and gentle as he cut off the bandage and removed the drainage tube. The fingers were curled, and the doctor said, "Straighten them."

"I don't think I can."

"This will hurt." The doctor began to uncurl the fingers, and Richard took a deep breath and tightened his stomach muscles. "Very much?"

Richard tried to smile. "Well, this hurts me more than it does you, Doctor."

The Italian grinned. "How far up? Here?" He explored the elbow.

Richard let out enough breath to say, "Yes."

The exploring thumb now went deep into the armpit. "This gland, is it sensitive?"

"Ouch!"

"That word must be the same in all languages." Now he examined the incision in the palm. "I am not happy about it. But you'll probably survive." He went on to say something in Italian medical terms which was completely outside the bounds of Richard's vocabulary. "All right," the doctor said, "I mean you have a kind of immunity to the sulfas, and if I give you this new antibiotic—which I know will knock the infection—it won't be safe for you to drive a car for nearly twenty-four hours. Affects your depth-perception, co-ordination, judgment—"

"Stop right there," Richard said. "What other flavors do you have?"

"When did you have penicillin last?"

"I don't know. Maybe a year ago."

"Not allergic to it?"

"Not that I know of."

"I hope not," Doctor Alciade said. When the syringe was ready, he said, "No use making a sore arm sorer. I'll give you a sore tail instead. Take down your pants, *signore.*"

Afterwards he came outside with Richard and walked up the street to the car with him. The expression on his face when he looked at the Ferrari made Richard suddenly realize that he liked this young, enthusiastic doctor very much.

"Yours?" Alciade breathed.

"Massimo's."

In a lost voice, the Italian said, "How many times I've wished—" He shook his head, smiling. "I drove the Mille Miglia once."

"You finished?"

Doctor Alciade looked straight at him and said, "Twenty-seventh," as if he were afraid Richard might laugh. It was nothing to laugh about; even to finish that horrifying thousand miles was a proud thing.

"I salute you," Richard said. "I ran out of road before Florence."

"Ah, but you will try again. I must not." He lifted Richard's bandaged hand. "Even so little a thing as this could end my career."

"I understand," Richard said. "I hope you will come to San Gregorio for the race."

"Oh, yes."

"Even better, why don't you come up to the festival tonight?"

"I have already thought of it!"

"I'll bet you have," Richard grinned.

"She will be there?"

Getting into the car, Richard said, "Wild horses couldn't keep her away."

"Nor me," said Doctor Alciade. He stood watching as Richard pulled out of the parking place, and then he walked out into the street to look after the car. Richard saw him in the mirror, so he let the engine rev up in low gear, and snapshifted into second, knowing he was leaving rubber tracks on the hot concrete, but also knowing how the flat bark of the exhaust would be like music to the tiny figure far back up the street.

He was almost out of the shopping district before he remembered Massimo, and had to turn around. The first novelty shop he went into provided buggy whips, but chains were harder to find, until he passed a jewelry store, where he completely lost his head.

There was a chain in the window, but it was not what Massimo had had in mind. It was antique filigree work, as delicate as a spiderweb, of gold studded with seed pearls, and it was attributed—according to the manager of the shop, although this of course could not be guaranteed—to Cellini.

Richard held the necklace in his good hand, and asked the price. When he was told, he walked out. He went around the block and came back. He had no intention of buying it, but it was the most beautiful thing he had ever seen; and because he so obviously appreciated it, the manager made a minute downward revision in price.

Before he entirely realized that he had agreed to take it, Richard found himself on the telephone to his bank in Rome, instructing them to deliver the cash to the jeweler's main store in the Piazza di Spagna. Then it was necessary to wait while the bank called the main store and explained, so that the main store could call this branch and authorize them to hand over the necklace to Richard. It was an hour before the money was delivered and the last phone call completed. The necklace had long since been placed in its velvet box and wrapped in waterproof silk. It made a very small parcel. Still a little stunned, Richard looked at the insignificant rectangle and said to the manager, "It cost as much as a Ferrari and it hasn't even got wheels."

He was thoroughly disgusted with himself, so he went to the nearest florist and bought an extravagant bouquet. Then he got into the car and drove back up the mountain, over the thirty-mile serpentine leading to San Gregorio. It was now nearly eleven o'clock, and there was considerable traffic on the winding road, so that it was impossible to make good time. Richard sat at the wheel, cold with rage at himself, as the Ferrari crawled in second gear, unable to pass the long line of trucks, until the road doubled back on itself around a dead-end canyon where he could see that nothing was coming the other way for at least a mile. He gunned the overheated engine, shifted into third, sounding the horn steadily as he swept past the slow traffic. They did not bother to pull over as he came through, and he found himself scraping the brush of the mountainside, but he got through into the clear.

Now he drove hard, and it was the kind of driving the car was built for; the rev counter needle stayed almost in one position as he shifted down going into the corners, and shifted upward again on acceleration out of the bend. Because it was right-hand drive, the injured hand had to hold the wheel without relief, since his left never relinquished the gear lever for more than a moment. He ignored the pain, punishing himself; and he went around unprotected curves, unmoved, in a manner that would have left him limp if he had been passenger instead of driver.

It was noon when he came into the piazza. From the sound, there were still several cars out on the circuit, but most of the racing machines were at their pits, or being pushed off to the garages. Richard stopped before the hotel. He hated to waste any more time, but neither did he care to be seen with the bouquet of flowers. As he was getting out of the car, Uncle Fausto came out of the hotel.

"Just the man I want to see," Richard said.

"Everybody's been looking for you. Thought you might have had an accident."

"Too much traffic on the road. Look, put these in your icebox, will you? And put this in the safe, if you've got one."

"Where the hell have you been?" said Angelo.

Richard turned to him. "Didn't Massimo tell you? I went town to the clinic to get this bandage changed, and—" Angelo was looking at the flowers and the gift-wrapped package, but Richard went on anyway—"then I got trapped behind some trucks on the way back up. Am I too late for practice?"

"Yes," said Angelo.

"God damn it," Richard said. "I'm sorry."

"But then, maybe you don't need it."

"I said I was sorry."

"I sent Giorgio out to practice in your place."

Richard's heart sank; unable to protest, he stared down at Angelo, waiting for the rest of it. Uncle Fausto, embarrassed, said hastily, "I will do as you ask, Ricardo," and went into the hotel.

Angelo smiled apologetically. "In my place, what would you have done? If it took all that time only to have the hand attended to, the hand must be serious, and therefore it would be safer to depend on Giorgio. You see?"

"That's crap. I'm a better driver than Giorgio, and you know it."

"True—when you are available," Angelo said, smiling.

Richard smiled, too. "You can be a real bastard."

"And you," Angelo said, "are a genuine jerk."

"I know it," Richard said. "Do you?"

"Of course, Ricardo. Do you still love me, anyway?"

"More than an enemy, less than a brother."

"At my age," Angelo sighed, "one is grateful for small favors. What was in the package?"

"Oh, just a—trinket."

"You're a bigger jerk than I thought. She doesn't want peace offerings, she wants you."

"What?"

"Jesus and Mary! You Americans can be naive."

"Do you mind telling me what the hell you're talking about?"

"Why else would she let Von Lutzow back in the saddle? I trust I'm not being indelicate—"

Weakly, Richard said, "Oh, I never thought of that." He was overwhelmed with relief, because last night at the coronation there had been a bad moment when he thought Angelo had looked inside him and seen the truth.

"You don't seem to care very much, one way or the other."

"I don't," he said easily. "There're too many runners in that race. Anyway, I didn't buy any peace offerings. The flowers are for Ghita, for tonight."

"And the—trinket?"

"For my next girl. You got any nice ones lying around loose?"

"Find your own girls," Angelo said.

"If you're not using that one you were with last night—"

"That one," Angelo said in a disgusted voice. "All promise and no performance. She has an exaggerated idea of the commercial value of chastity, which I'm positive she took leave of when she was five. Also she has a father who considers her a highly negotiable asset. Still—anything can happen tonight." He took Richard by the arm, "Why are we standing in the sun?"

"I can't leave the car here. It'll melt."

"Then put it away. I'll be at the *trattoria.*"

By the time he got there, there wasn't an empty chair under the olive tree, but again the Scuderia Barzio had the best location in the shade.

"Let the Little One sit on Ricardo's knee," said Angelo. "Anyone that small doesn't rate a chair to himself."

"Thanks for the car," Richard said. "I got what you asked for."

"What did I ask for?"

"Later." He sat down on the chair vacated by Massimo, who perched on his knee. "How went the machines?"

"Well," Angelo said. "But not well enough."

"What's the matter with them?"

"There is nothing wrong with the machines. It's the old women I have driving them."

Massimo and the Solferino brothers looked at each other and Giorgio said placidly, "Should we tell him that Enzo himself has signed us up for next season?" The others yelled with laughter, because it was a wonderful joke. Except for Massimo, they had less chance of being selected by the official factory team of Enzo Ferrari than they had of becoming king of Italy.

"Good," said Angelo, "I'll pay your salaries if Enzo will only take you off my hands."

"I'll tell him when I see him," Giorgio said. "Massimo made fastest lap. Two minutes, eight and a half. Von Lutzow did two-eleven. The noble English and one of the Gordini people tied with Felice at two-fourteen."

"And?"

"I did two-fifteen. I was saving it for you," Giorgio told him. "Can you improve on that this afternoon?"

"I'll try," Richard said, looking at Angelo. "Won't I, *padrone?*"

"If you're not too busy elsewhere."

"You're a sweet guy. Who's to beat? Von Lutzow?"

"The Gordini is dangerous."

"Jean Behra?"

"No," Massimo said. "Behra's still in the hospital from the Mexico crash. Some Englishman."

"American," said Giorgio.

"American?" Richard sat up. "Who?"

"Who knows?" asked Angelo. "Probably some kid that had a ride once in an MG, and it went to his head."

"Driving for Gòrdini? Come again," said Richard.

"Trying to muscle in on our sport. Let one American in, the next thing he brings all his relatives," Angelo said. "U.S.! Go home!"

"And who'd feed you," Richard said.

"We let you aid us so much we can last for years," Angelo said. "We won't need you again until after the next war."

"That's gratitude," Richard said. "What's the guy's name?"

"How long do you want us to be grateful?" Angelo said. "His name's Vollmer, or something."

"Charley Vollmer? I know him. We ran at Pebble Beach last year. I wonder what he's doing here."

"Driving for Gordini tomorrow," Angelo said. "You boys better form a union, before these rich Yankees take your jobs."

Richard flushed, but he wondered how Vollmer had made it. He looked around the café; Vollmer wasn't in sight, but Diana was very much in evidence, in the lowest-cut sports dress that had ever been seen in San Gregorio. She waved to him and said something with a laugh that Richard couldn't distinguish above the clamor of a hundred voices speaking excitedly in six languages. He waved back, noting the first smile he had seen on Von Lutzow's face, and turned back to his own group. Massimo was looking at Diana, and Richard knew what he was thinking.

"What of the queen?" Richard said.

Absently, Massimo said, "The women are fixing the dress she will wear tonight."

"I got a bouquet for you to give her. I thought maybe you wouldn't have time to get any flowers."

He couldn't take his eyes off Diana. "Yes . . . oh,

thanks. I forgot all about flowers. You can give them to her."

"No," Richard said flatly. "You will give them to her. Uncle Fausto's keeping them in the icebox."

"And I should have some flowers to give to your girl."

"The lady is not my girl," Richard said patiently.

"He said it in front of witnesses," Angelo said.

"She should learn Italian," Massimo said. "It is very difficult this way."

"There's Vollmer," Richard said suddenly. He pushed Massimo off his knee and went through the crowd. Vollmer saw him coming and his round face crumpled up in a delighted smile.

"Ya bum!" he yelled. Richard offered his left hand and they shook violently, much happier to see each other than they would have been at home. "What happened to the meathook?" Charley Vollmer demanded. "You crash?"

"Infected cut, nothing serious."

"Ya big bum," Charley said happily. "I been hoping to run into you for a month."

"So you're driving for the sorcerer, eh? Coming up in the world, aren't you?"

"Yeah," said Charley, punching him, "right up there with Ascari, Delgard and Fangio."

"Don't kid yourself, sonny," Richard told him. "This isn't the big league."

"Don't kid *me*," Charley said. "It's a *Grand Prix*—it's on the F.I.A. International Calendar—and what the hell was all that machinery I saw practicing this morning? A bunch of hot rods welded up in somebody's back yard?" He glared at Richard. "If this isn't big league, for Christ's sake, what is it?"

"Don't get sore, Charley."

"Well," Charley said, defensively, "it's good enough for me, even if it isn't good enough for you."

"That's the sad part," Richard said. "It's *just* my speed."

Charley looked at him with amazement. "What's with this modesty routine? Don't you think I can read? You've hardly missed a *Grand Prix* this year—you've raced against Ascari at least four times—"

"Charley, I doubt if Ascari was aware of the fact. The only time I ever saw him, between the starts and the finishes, was when he lapped me."

"Yeah, but—"

"Charley," Richard said. "You don't see Ascari here, do you? Or Fangio, or Gonzales, or Farina, Villoresi, Hawthorn, Manzon, Chiron, Rosier—"

"Oh, shut up," Charley said.

"Will it cheer you up if I introduce you to the successor of Nuvolari?"

"Yeah, who?"

"Teammate of mine. Funny little guy named Massimo—"

"Yeah, man!" said Charley. "I hear he's real hot. He around here now?"

"He was sitting on my lap a minute ago—there he is."

"My God," Charley said. "I thought that was somebody's little boy. When I saw him out on the circuit he didn't look like that."

"That little boy is as big a man as you'll ever meet."

"Well," Charley said generously, "I admit I couldn't lay a wheel on him. Funny, too, because the Gordini's perfect for this circuit. Running right, I'll bet it's five seconds per lap faster than the Ferrari. Still, I couldn't stay with him."

"When you figure out why, you get a lollipop. Come on."

He introduced Charley in English, then he said in Italian, "It is his first *Grand Prix,* and he feels very proud to meet real *Grand Prix* drivers."

Giorgio said, "Please, Ricardo. Do not say that where anyone might overhear." They all laughed, and Charley said, "What was that all about?"

Richard said, "I told them you said the Gordini is five seconds faster than the Ferrari—and Giorgio said it depends on who's driving the Gordini."

Charley blushed furiously. "Jesus, Dick, you want to ruin me with these guys, telling a thing like that?"

"Keep your shirt on—I'm only kidding. They were laughing at themselves."

The crowd was thinning out now as people drifted off to lunch, and suddenly there were plenty of chairs and even some hope of being waited on.

Charley said, "I never trust an American that can speak a foreign language, but I want you to tell Massimo that I'm happy to be driving in the same race with him. Now," he said nervously, "make it clear I didn't say I expect to give him any trouble—just in the same race, is all. You got that?"

Richard translated, complete with instructions. Massimo grinned. "Tell him I am happy, too. He drives very well. Very fast. Tell him that I consider him a serious threat, truly."

"A new love match," Angelo said in Italian. "You know he thinks the Gordini is faster than your machine?"

Richard translated Massimo's compliment.

"You're kidding?" Charley said, not daring to believe.

"So help me," Richard said.

"Jee-zuss," Charley said limply, not caring if his heart stopped right now.

"Tell him, also," Massimo prodded Richard, "that he is right about the Gordini."

"Are you crazy?" Richard said. "That would sound as if you were bragging. And it makes a bum out of the poor kid."

"Truly?" Massimo was puzzled. To him it was only a simple statement of fact, completely devoid of any personal connotation, because he thought of his driving ability as being as normal for him as having brown eyes.

"What's he say, what's he say?"

Seriously Richard said, "He says he hopes you enjoy being here with the team of Gordini, in his native village —Massimo's native village, not Gordini's; I don't know where Gordini's birthplace is, although it was in Italy somewhere, which is strange when you realize that Gordini, an Italian—although maybe he's a Frenchman now—is the hope of France in *Grand Prix* racing."

"He didn't say all that," Charley said.

"More or less. He sort of inferred it."

"Inferred-inschmerd," Charley said. "You're giving me the needle again."

In Italian, Angelo said, "Behind that cherubic visage lies an intuitive mind. He suspects you of treachery, and rightly."

"What's he say?"

"I said," Angelo spoke in English for the first time, "that if you ever need a mouthpiece, don't hire this ambulance-chasing shyster, or he'll doubletalk you into the electric chair for overtime parking."

"Let that be a lesson to you," Richard said righteously. "Never trust an American who talks a foreign language."

After lunch, Richard didn't know what to do with himself. The practice session would not begin until the heat of midday was past. Massimo had disappeared cliffward, Charley was off somewhere with the French contingent, and Angelo was at the garage with Giorgio and the mechanics. He thought of going there, too, but he had long ago learned that the most popular driver in the team was the one who stayed out of the mechanics' hair. He did not want to go back to his room. He explored himself for the pre-race tension that normally appeared twenty-four hours before the start, but it was not measurably there yet.

Finally, he went for a walk. The humpbacked bridge drew him, and for a time he leaned over the ancient, crumbling parapet and stared down at the trickle of water in the bottom of the ravine. He thought mechanically, and without emotion, about the bridge, imagining a number of unpleasant things that could follow a miscalculation, an act of carelessness, or just bad luck. He was not afraid of the bridge at this moment, but he respected it, and he was aware that he might be afraid again later.

He left the bridge and walked up through the S-curve to the bend, high on the mountainside, where the road leveled off and was called the Mountain Straight, although it ran in a long sweeping curve against the hollow flank of Monti di Belleri for almost a mile, constituting the only really fast section of the circuit.

Richard ambled along the road until he came to a place that brought into his line of vision the bridge, the street leading into the piazza, the pits, and the *trattoria*. He sat down with an olive tree and the road at his back, and looked at the village below him. The castle was on his left, and he glanced at it, wondering in what room Diana was lunching with the prince. It amused him to think how bored Geoffrey must be right now—interminable courses of food, limitless varieties of wine—when Geoffrey really preferred a bag of potato chips and a bottle of milk. He looked at the towers, wondering idly whether they were Gothic or Renaissance, or both, and not caring, but wondering in the back of his mind: In what room sleeps the queen this night? His glance swept across the village from left to right and he squinted at a small white house at the top of the stone stairway. The shutters were closed against the sun, or perhaps against prying eyes from the hillside.

He was conscious of an immense dissatisfaction with

everything, but primarily with himself. "All right," he said out loud, "now all we need is—" The answer did not come. It was an expression he had used for years, as a kind of trick to set the machinery of his mind in motion: Usually it worked; usually his consciousness threw off its sloth, leaped to attention and made a hopeful suggestion, like an eager child who has done his homework.

"The trouble is, ladies and gentlemen of the jury, the trouble is that I don't know what my trouble is." He examined that briefly, and decided that it represented some progress, if only in a negative sense.

He remembered the last thing Marian wrote in the letter when she decided to break with him: *Stop allowing yourself the luxury of despair* . . . He had snorted when he read it, because he didn't know what she meant, and suspected she didn't either, but now he was less sure . . .

Did she mean that he sought defeat, and took comfort in it? Is R. Delgard a champion of lost causes? Does he pretend to want only that which he is certain he cannot have? Ladies and gentlemen of the jury, let us look at the record, let us examine the causes for which he has waged a losing battle. Exhibit A: Motor Racing. Exhibit B: Diana. Exhibit C: Ghita. There are more, but these will suffice to prove the contention of the prosecution: that the defendant, Delgard, joins only those struggles which are safely lost in advance. Look closely at the exhibits offered in evidence, ladies and gentlemen. Could Delgard possibly reach the pinnacle, enter the charmed circle of the immortals of racing? Forgive me if I smile at such an absurdity. *And he knew it!* Could he have Diana, well and truly and forever? (Could any man?) Do I hear a titter among you? *And he knew it!* But, please, keep your minds open—there's still another: Ghita. Did Delgard think he had even a prayer with her? I beg the Court's indulgence for the jury's laughter at this absurdity. *And he knew it!*

You may well ask what motivates this windmill-tilter, this latter-day Don Quixote, this anachronism. I'll tell you: while mankind fights for a million personal victories, this product of an overactive pituitary has signed a pact of passive resistance with himself. He knows that to dare greatly, and to fail by a hair's breadth, would advertise the exact sum of his deficiencies. So, for camouflage, he pursues only the acknowledged impossibles, when the game is already lost when he comes on the field, and the odds against him insurmountable. But he fights the noble fight, with a courage greater than lions'—and loses, and is still safe, and unrevealed. Because, ladies and gentlemen of the jury—and with this I rest the case of Society versus Richard Delgard—if the cause is truly lost, no onus attaches to him who fights for it and fails, but instead a kind of sad glory, a luxurious despair . . .

Richard threw a stone down the mountainside and watched the little geysers of white dust that rose each place it touched. That hypothesis, he thought, could set psychiatry back twenty years. The hell with Marian, the hell with what she says—remember instead what Grandma, a much wiser old bird, always told you: "Thinking is bad for young men; the world is safer when they work with their hands." Grandma would like the necklace.

He turned over and made himself comfortable on the ground, in the shade. He tried not to think of anything, but just before he fell asleep, the thought crossed his mind: Still, that prosecuting attorney made mincemeat of me—and where are my medals to show he was wrong?

Chapter Eleven

H ow was lunch?" Richard called, as he passed the GRP pit.

Geoffrey looked up from tightening a fuel line. "Not bad," he said. "Bit much."

Hans looked over the pit counter. "Ah, Mr. Delgard."

Richard said amiably, "Herr von Lutzow."

"We will have the pleasure of your company this afternoon?"

"I trust it will be a pleasure."

Von Lutzow smiled and nodded, to show that he felt very kindly toward the world today. Richard went on down the line to the Scuderia Barzio pit. The three flaming-red machines were neatly lined up diagonal to the pit counter, with their noses pointing into the corner of the piazza where the course ran between the *albergo* and the castle wall. The Number Three machine had a newly painted band of white and blue—the racing colors assigned to the United States—encircling its nose.

"Why, Angelo, that's real sweet of you," Richard said. "But where's the U.S. Go Home?"

"Where you been? Thought you'd got lost again."

"Up on the hill. Under a tree. Asleep."

"With whom?"

"The prosecuting attorney," Richard said, taking his crash helmet, goggles and driving gloves off the seat of Number Three. He touched the dent and put the helmet on.

Giorgio and Felice appeared with a crate of Coca-Cola bottles, and at the same moment Massimo appeared, and they all helped themselves and stood around Angelo, who said, "For the benefit of this morning's absentees, I will repeat: no overtaking in the chute—the downhill section leading onto the bridge. No overtaking between the castle and the creek crossing—in other words, no passing anywhere in the lower town; not that I think any of you are crazy enough to try. Okay to pass from the bridge to the castle, and on all other sections not otherwise specified. Flag signals and pit signals as usual. Anyone who blows up an engine by revving over eight thousand can keep right on walking. I want to earn starting money, at least, for all three cars tomorrow, so don't overdo it today. Nevertheless, I expect you to qualify all three cars for the first row of the grid—although I might have to settle for one in the second. So don't drag your feet."

"What do you figure we have to do to cinch the pole positions?" Richard said.

"Most of the lap speeds should be a couple of seconds better this afternoon. Probably two minutes eight seconds for the Little One. If you and Felice do two-ten, that ought to give fastest laps." He looked at Massimo, who nodded soberly.

"All right," said Angelo. "Three laps to warm up. If the machines are ready at the end of the third, give the signal as you approach the pits, and the timers will be on you for the next three laps. If I'm satisfied, I'll bring you in then. Otherwise I'll wave you on until I am. Questions?"

"I might need an extra warm-up lap or two," Richard said.

"I'll be the judge of that," Angelo said flatly. "You just obey orders. I want you all to qualify and get off the circuit as soon as possible, before it gets cluttered up with the Sunday drivers. Anybody who doesn't qualify for either first or second row will have to go out and try again later, after we see what times the opposition has clocked." Nobody said anything, so Angelo added, "Get going on the flag."

The three red machines waited, trembling, their engines assaulting unprotected eardrums for a quarter-mile around. Then the green flag was flown above the timing stand, and the course was open. Massimo moved off cleanly, rear wheels spinning on the polished cobbles. Felice lurched ahead and stalled, so Richard let in the clutch and felt the Ferrari leap forward; he swung wide around Felice and took off after Massimo in a small series of tail slides. Fifty feet ahead, Massimo dove down out of the piazza, following the descending left-hand curve of the castle wall.

Richard's memory took over now; the large-scale map he had fixed in his mind that first morning now flowed past the back of his eyes, showing him the important details he could not see at even this moderate speed . . . the hitching-post is my braking point. Now bottom gear and not much slide and only a whisper of throttle. It's a right-hander into a narro v street with a doorstep just beyond that juts out two feet and could flip you. All right, you missed it very nicely, but don't waste time patting yourself on the back—just get set for the next one just like it, not forgetting the spot where it's always wet from the drains . . .

The corner came and he took it a trifle too fast, losing time correcting the slide, and then he was past the wet place, going well, but Massimo was already rounding the fast left-hander that led in a gentle curve to the creek crossing.

I've got to improve right now, Richard thought, because if I can't close up on him on this downgrade, he'll lose me forever on the long climb up the other side. Fifty feet this side of the open corner, Richard steered for the inside of the turn, touched the brakes lightly to break the rear end loose, added throttle to correct the slide into a four-wheel drift. Halfway through the curve he thought he was too fast to get around, but he sat like iron, holding it without flinching, and to his relief the machine held its line all the way through as if it were on rails. He straightened the wheel and pushed the throttle to the floor, and his hands were wet inside his gloves. But he was headed for the creek crossing with tremendous velocity, with Massimo's car getting larger every second.

Doing a hundred and five in third gear, he shot across the trickle of water, and the nose of the machine came up and he was climbing the mountain road in Massimo's wake. Halfway to the left-hander where the road leveled off, Richard knew that he would be nose-to-tail at the top of the climb, and they would go into the turn together.

As Massimo braked, and down-shifted for the corner, he threw a glance behind, and then a second time, because Richard was overtaking on the inside. Both cars were drifting now, perfectly, with Massimo going wider to give Richard room; but Richard had sacrificed too much speed in order to hold the short radius of the turn, and as they accelerated out of the curve, Massimo was already a length ahead.

Massimo looked back with a wide grin; he beat on the side of the cowling in sheer delight and violently waved Richard an invitation to overtake him. But it was not possible now and they both knew it. Here on the long, level, gentle left-hand sweep, Richard was paying the penalty for his size; his added weight and wind resistance made the appreciable difference. Massimo was pulling steadily away, three or four miles an hour faster.

Richard didn't care. He had never felt so exultant. I'm driving way over my head, he thought, and today is my day. Don't crow too soon, he checked himself—there is still the chute and that unmentionable bridge.

Again he managed to close the gap appreciably as he plunged down the chute after Massimo, although he knew in his heart that the Little One was not driving all-out, as Richard was. They went over the bridge only four car-lengths apart, cleared the building and swung into the street leading down to the pits in the piazza. Wherever it was downhill, Richard could pick up precious seconds, although they would have to be paid for later in tired brakes and threadbare tires; for he was not only going through the corners fast, but was making his approaches at higher velocity and leaving the braking until later than ever before in his career.

There were not two seconds between them as they went past the pits, and Richard caught a fleeting glimpse of Angelo putting both hands on his hips in a gesture of incredulity.

On the second lap, Massimo increased his speed, and Richard responded. This time he didn't try to overtake on the uphill straight after the creek crossing, but tucked in five feet behind Massimo and stayed there, letting the machine in front split the wind for him. They went through the top turn onto the Mountain Straight in that order, and when Massimo opened up for the full-speed stretch leading to the chute, Richard continued to slip-stream him, actually being drawn along by the partial vacuum in the wake of Number One.

If he could stay this close, not letting Massimo lose him on the straights, it would not be necessary for Richard to rush each corner so violently in an effort to close up. Nevertheless, he had to ease off in the chute, because it would have been insanity to hit the bridge this close behind Massimo. He dropped back twenty yards, went over the bridge easily, skidded less than usual, and caught up again with Massimo before they were through the piazza.

The third lap was faster, with Richard completely satisfied with his tactics. They had still seen no other cars on the circuit, although Felice, at least, must be out, somewhere behind them, because there was no sign of him at the pit when Massimo and Richard came into the piazza the third time, giving the okay signal with one hand, so that the timers would start clocking them officially.

It was as if Massimo had turned on a spare engine. Richard answered with everything he knew, but he realized that he was driving at the very limits of safety, whereas Massimo's car still seemed to have an appreciable margin of control in reserve—a condition which Richard attributed to the fact that his own Number Three was carrying at least a hundred pounds more weight than Number One, and was thus subjected to considerably higher centrifugal forces on the turns.

Once more he caught Massimo on the uphill climb, but only by plunging down across the ravine bottom at the absolute maximum that the engine was capable of to drag the car. Again he slipstreamed Number One, and could not be shaken off on the mile-straight. In the chute, he refused to back off. For a split second, both cars were actually in the air at the same time, and the crash of Number One landing was echoed instantly by the landing of Number Three. The wall of the building looked like an overhanging cliff as they brushed past it and slid through the last turn leading down toward the pits.

Richard had no idea what the lap time could be, but he knew that it was very fast, and he also knew that he could not maintain this pace for the next two laps.

He was sure of it when Massimo left him standing in the lower town on the second timed lap, piling up so big a lead, on the corners, that Richard was unable to catch him on the climb. Still trying as hard as before, he watched Number One going away on the Mountain Straight, and he thought: I've lost the edge, I couldn't sustain it. Massimo was already on the bridge as Richard was only turning down into the chute. They crossed the piazza separately for the first time, with Massimo out of sight around the castle turn when Richard came into view of the pits.

This time he overtook a Maserati on the uphill section, and passed both Geoffrey and Von Lutzow coming onto the Mountain Straight. He beat one of the Gordinis into the chute by leaving the braking until the last second, but Massimo was not even in sight. Richard fled through the

S-curve, took the bridge with a jolt that made his teeth ache, somehow missed the building, and slammed down toward the finish line. This time he didn't ease up and hit the brakes until he was past the timing stand, and he barely got around the castle turn.

He had done his best, and it had just not been good enough, after that first timed lap. Feeling terribly let down, as though he had discovered something rather shameful about himself, he toured slowly around the course, letting the engine cool down gradually. He stayed well over to the right in order not to balk the fast cars; and because he wanted to postpone what he knew awaited him at the pit, he went slower and slower. Eight cars passed him on the Mountain Straight, and then both GRP's passed him a second time as he coasted down into the piazza.

Number One was up on the jacks with all the wheels off, so the mechanics could examine the spokes, the tires, and the brake linings; the hood had also been lifted off, and Angelo was watching Giorgio remove the spark plugs. Richard pulled in alongside and cut the switch, looking for Massimo, whom he discovered inside the pit, pouring a dipper of water over his head.

Richard took off his helmet and goggles, and carefully peeled the glove off his bandaged hand. Nobody had said anything to him, or acknowledged his presence by more than a glance.

Sitting in the car, Richard said, "Remember me?"

They all looked at him with the same curious expression.

Angelo said, "Was she turning up properly?"

"Yes."

"No mechanical trouble at all?"

"Look," suggested Richard, "you skip the sarcasm, and I'll skip the alibis. She went perfectly. I went all right, too—for one lap."

"Oh?"

"Yes, oh!" Richard said, getting mad.

"And what do you think was wrong with the other two laps?"

"Like I said. The first was okay. I just couldn't keep it up."

"Go on," Massimo said, scrubbing his head with a towel. "Why don't you tell him how lousy he was?"

Angelo looked at a slip of paper. "Lap times were two

minutes nine seconds, two-seven and one-fifth, two-six flat. Breaks the course record."

Richard said to Massimo, "Congratulations, runt. Don't bother mentioning my times."

They all looked at each other and began laughing. Massimo said, "*Those* are yours, you unspeakable idiot."

"I don't understand," Richard said, utterly bewildered.

"Who does," said Angelo. "Massimo did two-nine, two-six, two-three and three-fifths."

"The clocks must be wrong," Richard said flatly. "You mean I improved each lap?"

Angelo handed him the official tape from the electric timers. Richard stared at it for a while, then he said weakly, "I'll be a sad son of a—I drove that fast?"

They laughed at him again, and Massimo brought him an ice-cold Coke, and the others made a great business of assisting him out of the Ferrari, as if he were something very fragile and very valuable. Richard, marveling, was embarrassed, but happy; and then the joke stopped when Giorgio said, "Here comes Felice—lap time fifteen minutes."

Felice was on foot, hot and dirty and angry. The magneto drive had sheared and Number Two was parked on the Mountain Straight. The two mechanics started for the bridge immediately; they would have to push the machine for half a mile, but after that they could coast all the way in. Giorgio began checking through the spare parts to make sure he had everything ready, while Richard sat with Angelo and Massimo on the pit counter and watched the other qualifying cars streak through the piazza. He had the timing tape in his hand, and he kept looking overtly at it, thinking: This ought to make a bum out of the prosecuting attorney. . . .

Charley Vollmer went by on one of the Gordinis, followed by two of the Veritas derivatives of the pre-war BMW, then another Gordini, two Cooper-Bristols, driven by the Englishmen, Pollock and Bittersweet, and then the Maserati Richard had seen earlier. This was followed almost at once by two more Maseratis with a very different exhaust note, although externally the three cars appeared identical.

"Jesus and Mary," Massimo said, "did you notice?"

"I'm wondering the same thing," Angelo said, looking worried.

"What's the matter?" Richard said.

"Maserati's got a very fast new two-liter engine. Six cylinder, twelve plugs, but the factory's not entered for this race—all the Maseratis are listed by private entries."

"Those last two are six-cylinder," Massimo said.

"A sneak preview," Richard said in English.

"It may be. New engines and chassis with the old bodies, so that if they don't do too well, only the so-called private owners are blamed. It's been done before, and it's a cute trick when it works." Angelo got off the pit counter and strolled toward the timing stand. Charley Vollmer came into the piazza and stopped at his pit. Massimo said, "I think I will go call on an old friend, who happens to be driving a Maserati, of all things." He jumped down from the counter, grinning at Richard.

"You're not the only one with friends," Richard said. They went in opposite directions along the line of the pits.

As Richard approached, Charley was just climbing out of the bright blue Gordini, saying to the men around him, "Very fast on the straights," illustrating with his hands. "Passed everything I saw. But the rear end seems light. Breaks loose too soon in the turns—whoosh! Too much wheelspin for good acceleration . . ." Richard stood close enough to listen, while pretending to be engrossed in the passing parade of racing machines. Charley was discussing the possible value of undergearing the rear axle and using larger rear wheels; this would give slightly more tractive surface of rubber, and a certain amount of weight increase where it seemed to be needed. He saw Richard and said, "A spy!"

"Come along and have a Coke," Richard said.

"Don't go away," Charley said. He got out of the car and came over to Richard, and they walked back to the Ferrari pit.

When he had given the younger man a soft drink, Richard said, "What kind of time you put up?"

"Two-nine, about," Charley said. "Hear Massimo clocked under two-four."

"Yes," Richard said. "Of course, he wasn't really trying."

"Do tell!" Charley said. "I'll spot him a hundred yards on the Mountain Straight and still beat him to the end of it."

"Do tell," Richard said politely. "Too bad the whole course isn't like the Bonneville Salt Flats."

"There you have me, chum," Charley said. "He'll murder me in the lower town, unless . . ." He decided to change the subject. "Man, there's a couple Maseratis out there that are wolves in sheep's clothing. How'd they ever get all that speed out of those old engines?"

"Maybe they're powered by rubber bands," Richard said.

"Wait'll *you* try to take them." Charley was scornful.

"Just because they ran away from you," Richard said.

"They did like hell," Charley said indignantly. "I passed them both on the Mountain Straight. And *they* were trying, brother."

He saw Angelo coming back from the timing stand, so he said, "Sorry, kid, if you've finished your Coke, I've got work to do."

"I get the hint," Charley said. "Listen, what about this shindig tonight? Christ, I got no tuxedo!"

"Don't worry about it. Big racing drivers are expected to be eccentric. But wear a tie, if you own one—this isn't California."

Charley left and Richard waited for Angelo and Massimo, who arrived just as Number Two rolled silently down into the piazza, Giuseppe at the wheel, Tullio riding perched on the tail. Giorgio and the mechanics went to work at once.

"This is not going to be any walkover," Angelo said. "One of the Maseratis clocked two-five, and the best Gordini was only two-tenths of a second slower."

"It was like I thought," Massimo said. "They're the new six-cylinder cars, all right."

Richard said, "The Gordinis are having suspension troubles. Not enough rear-wheel adhesion. So they must be going like a bat out of hell on the Mountain Straight to turn a lap at that speed."

"If they can cure that," Felice said, "they will be very difficult to beat."

"Don't forget the Maseratis," Massimo said. "I think they will go out again. They want the front row tomorrow."

"When they do, you'll be with them," Angelo said, with decision. "I want comparative times for the section from the creek crossing to the chute. I don't care about the rest—nobody is faster across the bridge and through the lower town, but I am worried about the other."

"You want me out again, too?" Richard said.

"No, you and I are taking a walk. Felice stays here until Number Two is ready to qualify. Massimo waits until the Maseratis go out—"

"The Gordinis will try again, too," Richard said. "They're trying bigger wheels."

"All the better; we'll clock them, too."

"I didn't stay in the front row very long," Richard said.

"Felice may make it," Angelo said, but he was thinking about something else.

"I wouldn't mind having another crack at it," Richard persisted.

"No," Angelo said, and Richard didn't argue any more.

They took a pair of stop watches and walked up across the bridge, staying up on the bank at the side of the road as they climbed the chute. There was nothing important practicing now except Geoffrey's cars. Von Lutzow went past them, looking very fast and sounding healthy, but Geoffrey's own mount was sitting in a pool of oil at the end of the Mountain Straight. They went over to him. Geoffrey had been under the car, and now he stood up, soaked in oil, and looked haggard.

"Hello, chaps."

"What happened?"

"Don't know, really. Something seized, crankshaft broke. Looks like spaghetti inside."

"You got a spare engine?" Richard said.

"Old one."

"If there's any way we can help," Angelo said, "let me know."

"You have machine tools in your van?"

"Yes," Angelo said. "If you want any help, let me know right after practice closes, and before the bloody fiesta begins again."

"Decent of you," Geoffrey said, forlornly.

They went along the road until they found a place where they could see, far below on their left, the creek crossing, and on their right, but only a little below where they stood, the curve which marked the entrance to the chute.

"I want you to take the first one that appears. From the moment he hits the water down there, to the time he is clear of that tree—the bent one at the head of the chute. Where's the flag marshal?"

"Ain't no such animal," Richard said. "There's a flag-man just before the water splash, and one at the top of the climb by the escape road, and another at the bend at the end of this straight, but nobody at the top of the chute."

"Blessed Jesus," Angelo said. "The one place where they're needed. What happens if somebody piles up on the bridge, and there's no one to flag down the cars coming down the chute?"

"Like Geoffrey said. Spaghetti."

"What the hell's the matter with all you drivers? Why didn't you report it? Don't you know it might be your own neck?"

"Sorry," Richard said.

"You might be," Angelo said.

"You want me to go down now and—"

"I need you here." They sat down on a patch of wiry grass, and for a while neither of them said anything. Finally Angelo, said, in a better humor, "I wish we'd brought a bottle of wine."

"Yeah. And I could use a bacon, lettuce and tomato sandwich on white toast."

"A nation of drugstore gourmets," Angelo said.

"You should talk. If it isn't made out of library paste or soaked in olive oil until it's unrecognizable, you can't eat it."

"As a patriot, I resent that. The difficulty is that I am composed of equal parts of patriotism and intelligence—which prevents me from being outstanding in either department. What you say has a degree of truth, but like most generalities, it is guilty of oversimplification. Would you care to hear me generalize on the standard of cooking in your wonderful country?"

"I've got plenty of time," Richard said.

"Outside your famous restaurants, the food is fit for goats."

"I have a cousin who eats nothing but birdseed," Richard said.

"You see?"

"An Italian cousin," Richard said.

"Obviously the type who will migrate," Angelo said. "Here they come—you ready?"

"I'll take the first," Richard said.

They saw the Maserati hit the water splash, and Richard squeezed the button that started the sweep hand. A few moments later the second Maserati appeared. They watched them all the way around to the bent tree at the top of the chute, where they stopped their respective watches, read off the times and wrote them in Angelo's notebook. While they were doing that one of the Gordinis sneaked across the water splash before they could catch it. "Next time around for him. Now watch for Massimo." He had hardly said it before Massimo appeared. They waved as he went by, and he lifted a hand from the wheel in salute. "He's using all there is," Richard said.

"I can hear, too," Angelo said. Massimo went through the fast bend at the end of the straight and came back toward them, but lower down the mountain to the head of the chute.

"He's two seconds slower than the slowest Maserati," Angelo said. "If we raise the gear ratio for more top speed we lose our advantage over the bridge and in the lower town."

Another Gordini appeared, and this time they were ready. It was Charley Vollmer; he looked faster than any of them, and the stop watch confirmed it. The two Maseratis came through again, improving their times only fractionally; then the first Gordini reappeared, but he was misfiring as he climbed, so they did not bother timing him. Massimo was next. He passed the ailing blue machine on the straight and went into the sweeping turn at the end at what looked like an impossible speed, and an equally impossible angle of drift. But he got around and came back toward the chute.

"Better," Angelo said, "by a second. But still slower than the Gordini."

"I've got Charley," Richard said.

"I've got Felice—at last," Angelo said.

Charley was climbing full-bore, and Felice was grimly holding on fifty yards behind, until they were both on the Mountain Straight. Then, gradually, the French machine widened the gap. As he passed them, Richard said, "He must be turning a hundred sixty—not kilometers, *miles.*"

They watched him round the bend at the end of the Mountain Straight, which he managed almost as fast as

Massimo, but less steadily. Felice slammed past them in a rush of sound, and Richard had to drag his attention away from the Ferrari, to find Charley Vollmer just starting to drift into the head of the chute . . .

. . . Richard screamed: *"Look out!* Oh, no, no, no—" And he started to run, although it had scarcely happened yet. At the head of the chute a small child, a bunch of flowers in his hand, suddenly popped up from the ditch and had started across the road just as Charley appeared halfway around the turn in a fast, controlled slide. Petrified, the child stopped, rooted, in the center of the road; Richard, running, still seeing it happening *now,* seeing Charley correct the slide to avoid hitting the child, turning the wheel in the only direction he could and the machine whipping out of the controlled drift and hurtling out over the edge of the mountain . . .

Richard stopped . . .

The bright blue car glinted in the sun as it turned, so slowly, end over end, in midair . . . then, landed, far down the side of the ravine, and bounded into the air again, flipping over fast now. Charley lay where the car first touched . . .

Richard ran again, not on the road now, but down the steep side of the mountain above the chute, and he was vaguely aware that Felice had stopped on the turn and was getting out of the red machine, and running to the edge. Richard fell several times on the steep, rocky hillside, and his lungs ached painfully by the time he stumbled onto the road. But here he was balked, because the drop was sheer for a hundred feet, and for a frantic moment he could not think how to get down into the ravine without first going all the way to the bridge.

Felice grabbed him by the arm and hung on. "Don't go down there," Felice said, his voice shaking. "Oh, Holy Mary, Mother of Jesus! Did you see the way—"

An ambulance, looking and sounding like a toy from here, sounded its warning hooter, and appeared at the water splash to turn up the ravine, bouncing violently along the creek bed. People were hanging out the windows of the houses overlooking the ravine, pointing; scores of others materialized from below the bridge and around the corner of the piazza; hundreds splashed along in the wake of the ambulance.

"It is better not to see—there is nothing you can do—

it is better not to see," Felice said, the words coming out
in little bursts. He suddenly made a noise like a hurt animal, and ran back to the bent tree and retched.

Richard just stood there. He saw the ambulance halt
when it could go no further. Then the stretcher bearers
ran ahead, clawing their way up the rocky slope toward
where Charley lay, in his bright blue coveralls, like a
bundle of dirty laundry. Then all that could be seen was
a cluster of people, and nothing seemed to be happening;
finally the swarm of ants parted and the white uniforms
were carrying the stretcher very slowly to the ravine bottom where the ambulance waited. With the villagers assisting at every step, they reached the bottom and put
Charley into the ambulance; it had to go in reverse all the
way back to the creek crossing, with a hundred people
yelling directions, but at last it was on the road, the hooter
sounding its off-key, alternating note, going through the
lower town, and heading down the mountain. Richard saw
it once, through a fold in the hills, and it seemed to be
crawling, although he knew it was not; and the sound
of the hooter floated across the valley, faintly: *weeee-
waaahh-weeee-waaahh* . . .

Angelo said, "If they are rushing him to the hospital,
there must be a chance."

"Oh, God," Richard said, "why wasn't there a marshal
there?"

Angelo said, "We are all to blame."

And we can wallow in our guilt, Richard thought, but
he did not say it. He started walking down the chute.
He heard footsteps behind him and knew it was Angelo,
although the Italian made no attempt to catch up. Before crossing the bridge they looked back up the hill, and
saw Felice coasting down silently in Number Two without
having started the engine. When the Ferrari had rolled
over the bridge, they walked across it and down into the
piazza, going around behind the pits and up the steps of
the church.

Inside, he gave the old woman the first bill his fingers
touched, a thousand lire, for two candles. These he lighted
from the altar candles, and placed one at the feet of the
Virgin, and the other before the statue of the patron saint
of the village. Then, for a time, he simply stood there in
the dimness. Eventually, it seemed to him that he should
kneel, so he did. He said, "Please—it doesn't seem quite

fair for him to die that way, but if he has to, let him go easily."

As he went toward the door, he saw for the first time that many other drivers were kneeling, too, and many of the villagers. Angelo stood up, genuflecting and crossing himself, as Richard passed, and followed him outside.

Richard stood blinking in the brightness, and Angelo came up to him and said, "I didn't think you were Catholic."

"I'm not anything," Richard told him.

"Was he?"

"I don't know what he was," Richard said. "But just on the off chance."

They saw Felice coming toward the church. Angelo looked at his watch, and then across the piazza to where the green flag flew again above the timing stand. Felice caught the look.

"There is still time for thee to qualify," Angelo said softly.

"I know," said Felice. He was very subdued and pale. "I will only be a minute. May I borrow a little money?"

Angelo handed him a bill, and Felice went into the church, wiping his hands on the soiled, faded coveralls. When he was gone, Angelo touched Richard on the arm and they walked to the hotel and sat down in the back corner of the bar.

Without thinking about it, he knew that Angelo was afraid he might get drunk, so he drank the Strega very slowly, not wanting to cause any more pain than there was already.

In a few minutes Massimo came in and sat down facing Richard. He waited until Richard looked at him, then he said, "I was there, Ricardo. I helped, for thee. There was no mark on him. I swear it is true."

Richard wet his lips. "I am glad to know. What did the doctors say?"

"They did not know. He was in a coma."

"Where did they take him?"

"The Hospital of the Sacred Heart. The clinic is part of it," Massimo said. "I will have a Strega with thee . . . Felice is out on the circuit," he said to Angelo, "but I do not think he will be very fast."

"It cannot be helped."

"Can we telephone the hospital, and ask—"

Massimo said, "They have promised to call the hotel if there is any change."

The time went slowly. The bar gradually filled up, and there was much conversation about the accident. Many reasons were volunteered, but they were all wrong, so that it became apparent that only Richard and Angelo and Felice knew about the child. Angelo got up. "I had better tell the race committee what really happened, and stop all this crazy talk." He went out of the bar.

"Then it was not an accident," Massimo said.

"He knew what he was doing," Richard said.

"Ah," Massimo said, and it was enough.

Richard was glad that Angelo had gone, because he did not want to talk to him. The *padrone* was all right, but he was not a driver. With Massimo, it was another matter, because he understood that what Charley had done was of a certain value, and there were no words that could reach anywhere near it.

Felice came in and sat with them. "I went badly," he said. "I am sorry, Little One."

"It is of no importance, if thee at least qualified."

"Yes, that. Barely."

Massimo touched him on the shoulder. "Have a drink."

"I could not lift it," Felice said. "The hands are still trying to—"

Massimo lifted the drink. "Take it, man. I remember thee from the affair of the bridge. I was the first to reach thee when the Alfa stopped rolling over, but I was too small to lift it off thee, and thee smiled at me and said, 'Do I have to wait until you grow up?' "

Felice was looking at him and his face was very white. Massimo sat there holding the glass and he finally said, "But I am still too little, Felice. You'll have to lift it yourself."

After a moment, Felice reached out and took the glass from Massimo, held it and looked at it. No one said anything. There was only a faint tremor that jiggled the liquor in the glass. Felice took a delicate sip and put the glass on the table.

Uncle Fausto looked in the bar, saw them, and came over. He was already dressed for the banquet, except for the frock coat and the mayor's sash, which he would put on at the last minute.

"Ricardo, I have taken the flowers out of the icebox, for fear they would freeze."

"If you will take them when you go," Richard said to Massimo, who nodded.

"You want them now?" Uncle Fausto said.

"I would be grateful. And the little box."

When Uncle Fausto returned, Richard stripped off the wrapping and opened the velvet case. He held up the necklace. "This is a present for my grandmother, who is a wonderful woman. She would feel honored to know that it had been worn by a queen who was the friend of her grandson, and the fiancée of her grandson's friend."

Massimo looked levelly at him. He took the necklace and stared at it, turning it over carefully in his thin fingers. He passed it to Uncle Fausto, who also treated it reverently before letting Felice hold it. When it came back to Richard, he put it in the box and closed the lid.

"Thee will ask Ghita to do this favor for me tonight?"

They looked at each other thoughtfully, and Massimo said, "It would come better from thee."

"Will thee do as I ask?"

"Yes, Ricardo."

"Good. I won't be there tonight. I want to go down the mountain now."

"I understand," Massimo said quietly. "Take my car."

They walked around to the garage together. The three racing machines had been brought in and the mechanics were wiping them off. They looked at Richard, but said nothing. Massimo stood there holding the flowers and the velvet case as Richard folded himself into the car.

"Ricardo."

"Yes."

"I thank thee. For her."

"It's nothing." He saw the buggy whips, and he picked them up with an expression of distaste and threw them into a corner of the garage. Massimo said nothing. "Tell Angelo not to worry. I'll be back."

"We will light a candle for your friend."

"That's good."

Richard started the engine, and went out of the garage. As he drove slowly through the piazza, passed the hotel and turned the car onto the valley road, the village band was already warming up for the fiesta.

Chapter Twelve

Iᴛ ᴡᴀs almost nine o'clock when Richard returned to San Gregorio with Doctor Alciade, and the crowd was so dense he had difficulty driving through to the garage.

"The doors are locked," the doctor said.

"We'll have to leave it in the alley."

"It will be safe enough, if they know it is the property of Massimo."

Walking up the alley, Doctor Alciade took Richard's arm. "Try not to let yourself feel too sad."

"I can't feel anything," Richard said. "Just empty."

They pushed through the yelling, singing mob in the piazza, many hands pulling at them in invitation to the fete, but they freed themselves with smiles and went on to the hotel.

"All have gone to the castle, signori," said the boy doing duty at the reception desk; but he was wrong, because just then Angelo came out of the bar, wearing a cream silk dinner jacket. Richard introduced him to Doctor Alciade.

"You can get him into the party, can't you, Angelo?"

"Of course," Angelo said. "But you'd better get dressed in a hurry. You can't go in those coveralls."

"I'm not going," Richard said.

"What are you going to do?"

"Wash and eat and go to bed." It was not strictly true, but it was all he felt like saying.

"That will disappoint several people," Angelo said, "and it will not help Charley."

The doctor looked impatient, watching out the doorway, snapping his fingers in time with the band.

"I am very sorry that your friend is dead," Angelo said.

"You knew?"

"I telephoned down," Angelo said. "But I have told no one. It would only spoil the night. For Ghita, for the village. They will know and soon enough."

He wanted to be angry at Angelo, but it was not there. His intention was to write a letter to Charley's family—if he had one—because he thought they should know that Charley's life had not been snatched away from him, but

121

had been given deliberately, in exchange for another life, a transaction which would not be apparent in the official letter that would be written from the embassy, or in the half-dozen lines buried in the sports section of the newspapers.

"She is wearing the necklace, as you asked," Angelo was saying. "She was very proud to wear it, but there was not much joy because you would not see it on her. What is all this about, Ricardo?"

In English, Richard said, "I hardly know, myself. If I did, I still wouldn't discuss it with you."

"After tomorrow, what you do is your own business. Don't do anything foolish in the meantime," Angelo said, but he spoke so quietly there was no sting in the words. "You will come, then?"

"Yes," Richard said. "Go on ahead."

"We will wait. In the bar." He explained briefly to the doctor in Italian. Alciade said, impatiently, "Don't get that new bandage wet."

When he was ready, they pushed through the square and showed their invitations to the *carabinieri* stationed at the drawbridge; then they crossed the moat and went under the portcullis, where one of the two servants in livery and white wigs led them up a vaulted passageway, across the open terrace, and up a broad outside stairway that spiralled upward to the great hall of the castle.

Prince Vittorio saw them enter and hurriedly crossed to them, reflections from the candlelight glancing off the jeweled sunburst he wore on the left breast of his tailcoat; a wide red ribbon slanted across his evening shirt, and another decoration dangled from a blue ribbon around his neck. He looked like an actor made up for the role of Louis Napoleon.

With deep concern, Vittorio asked, "What of the young driver?"

"No change," Angelo said.

Vittorio's face showed his relief. "I was so afraid—" He looked around at his guests. "It would be a disaster," he murmured absently. "Come, come, I must present you to the queen." Crossing the room he whispered to Angelo, "But, my dear, she is exquisite, and I am furious with you for not having brought her to my attention years ago. To think that she has been right here—for the asking, one might say!"

"Already you are unfaithful to the English lady?"

"Don't be an idiot, my dear. She is equally delicious, but rather charmingly complicated. It is a different matter, altogether. The other one practically belongs to me."

"She might not agree. She is the fiancée of Massimo."

"You are an idiot! If I offered her my protection—" He did not think it necessary to finish the sentence.

Ghita was sitting on a dais at the end of the room, and the crowd was so thick around her that she was invisible until they were close enough to bow and kiss her hand.

Her eyes found Richard's, and he was not aware of anyone else in the room. The gown she wore was very old, of ivory velvet, studded with flashing stones; she wore long gloves of Florentine lace, and her hair was piled on top of her head, surmounted by the small golden crown. Her shoulders and throat were bare, except for the Cellini necklace of pearls, glowing against the dark, velvety skin.

Richard kissed her hand. Ghita said, "Thy friend, Ricardo?"

"There is no change," he said, guarding his expression. "I pray for him," Ghita said.

"Thank you." His face softened a little as he said, "I think Cellini had thee in mind when he created that necklace."

She touched it reverently with her gloved fingertips, and was about to reply to him, when suddenly as their glances met and held for a moment, something startled her—it was there for an instant in her eyes, and she took a quick breath and lowered her glance.

"I think it must be sinful to be so happy when sadness is so close," she said.

"I do not think so," Richard said. "They are never very far apart."

"Then," she said, her eyes levelly meeting his, "I am very happy that thee has come."

The others were crowding in now, impatient to claim her attention, and he turned away. Liveried footmen were passing through the assemblage with trays of drinks and canapes, and Richard took a glass of champagne and stood surveying the room. The vast expanses of pink marble were broken up by brocade paneling and tapestries; there were statues in alabaster and marble and gilded bronze, and all along the walls were niches with oversize busts of Vittorio's ancestors. A forest of giant candelabra illuminated the scene, which was watched over benevolently by a squadron of angels hovering in the peeling frescoes of the ceiling. Richard sipped the champagne and then exchanged it for a Scotch and soda, and crossed the room to where there was another dense cluster of people.

He was right. Diana was holding court, too, and Massimo was with her. She sat on a couch between Massimo and Von Lutzow, while Geoffrey stood leaning against the baroque carving of the fireplace, absently gnawing an olive. When Richard appeared, Diana immediately held out her hand for him to kiss, but he only shook it instead.

"Darling," she said, with laughter in her voice, "you'll have to forgive me—of course I'd have brought my damned coronet if I'd known."

"You seem to be doing all right without it," Richard said.

"Darling, you mean this simple little rag is really all right?"

"That simple little Dior rag?" he said.

"Balmain," she said, reproving him. It was a severe black cocktail dress, and its simplicity must have cost eight hundred dollars. There was no ornamentation on it at all, so that nothing took the attention away from the contrast of black silk and the rosy-tan skin and golden hair, although for anyone who needed to be reassured of her financial status, she wore a diamond bracelet that was two inces wide. Now that he could look at Diana objectively, Richard realized that she was as perfect a representation of Nordic beauty as Ghita was of the Latin, so that it was not surprising that she should have such an overwhelming effect on the locals.

"It's very becoming," Richard said. "Hello, Massimo."

"You have seen Ghita?" Massimo asked.

"Magnificent."

"Yes, yes," Massimo said, his eyes gleaming, but his glance kept flicking at Diana, and he had a pained look, as of terrible hunger. On the other side of Diana, Hans von Lutzow missed nothing, but he looked very sure of himself.

"I had to leave the car in the alley. The garage was locked."

"What is the news?" Even Massimo avoided using Charley's name.

"No change," Richard said.

"Dicky, what is being said?" Diana said insistently. "Dicky!"

He translated briefly and Diana said, "I'd have driven down with you, but you seem to have been avoiding me today, darling."

"I brought back a replacement. Another admirer for your string."

For a moment she let anger show in her face, but it dissolved almost as fast as it came. "You lamb," she said. "Who is it?"

"Doctor Alciade," Richard said, beckoning at the doctor, who was searching the crowd. He saw Richard above all the other heads and his face glowed as he pushed through to them.

It's wonderful, Richard thought, the way she is able to do it. Towering over the group, it was as though he sat in the balcony, watching a play in which one woman compelled—by sheer animal magnetism—the attention of this widely assorted group of males, promising each that he was secretly the favored, surmounting even the language barrier with a glance, a smile, or a discreet hand touching a knee as if to say, ". . . You . . ." Richard was not immune to it, either, but it no longer had the power to make him unhappy. Already she belonged to yesterday, and although he had no prevision of the tomorrows, he was at least faced in the direction of morning, and there was no urge to look over his shoulder. After a while he left the group, knowing she would never forgive him.

He went directly to Ghita, and, ignoring Angelo and the prince, he said, "I brought you a glass of champagne. It's thirsty work, being a queen."

Ghita said, "I have already said no a hundred times, but thee I cannot refuse."

"I underestimated you," Angelo said to Richard.

Then he shrugged at Vittorio, who said sardonically, "Youth calls to youth."

What he neglected to add was: But age has the last word. Comprehending, Ghita blushed, and for the first time Richard suspected how much anger she was capable of. Her voice was still quiet, but it shook with the effort of control, as she said, "You are an evil man, Signor Barzio. Because Signor Delaguardi has honored me by letting me wear the necklace of his grandmother, you would cheapen my gratitude—"

"My dear child," Prince Vittorio said; he put his hand paternally on hers. "My dear child," and his voice was just the right compound of gentle tolerance and amusement, so that it made Ghita look like a child unsuccessfully masquerading as one of her elders.

Angelo said, "It was only a joke, *cara*. In bad taste, perhaps—but still only a joke."

Her instinct seemed to tell her that they were being false, and Richard watched her struggle, and retreat, as the peasant nearly always retreated in the face of *droit du seigneur*. "I am a foolish girl, Angelo." But it was clear that she did not believe it, and they had won only a diplomatic victory. Richard was as pleased with her as if she had imperiously ordered them from the castle.

Vittorio looked equally pleased with her, and Richard thought he knew why. The queen would be sleeping in the tower tonight, and the true prince would doubtless honor her with a visit. Richard supposed there would be secret panels communicating with Vittorio's apartment, and he had a wild urge to find a sword and hide behind the draperies in her room, the way it always happened in the movies. He could see himself dueling with Vittorio, leaping across the bed, then out the window, blades clashing as they fought along the battlements. It was so silly he grinned a little, and his worries for her seemed suddenly absurd.

They dined in the room below the salon. It was almost as vast, and it needed to be, because a hunderd and twelve people sat down to dinner at the T-shaped table. Vittorio sat on Ghita's left at the top of the table, with Diana next to him and then Uncle Fausto, and the village council and their wives. Geoffrey sat moodily on the right of Ghita, and beyond him were the members of the race committee whose club sanctioned the coming event. Where the leg of the T joined the top, Angelo, Massimo, Richard and the Solferinos were seated, and beyond them stretched another twenty yards of banquet cloth, and the remainder of the racing teams, their wives and their girls, and the otherwise privileged.

There were endless courses, toasts and speeches, and nothing that was said was new or particularly worth listening to. Richard drank sparingly, feeling Angelo's watchful eye on him and the others. He felt the attention of both Diana and Ghita caressing him like fingers, but he had been pulled too far in too many directions recently, and he was losing his resilience. Now he was tired, and tomorrow was the race, and after that— He was tired, and the fear was beginning, and he was full of Charley now. . .

"What?" he said blankly.

"I asked," Vittorio patiently repeated, "what is your impression of Italy, Signor Delaguardi?"

"I like it," Richard said guardedly, but they expected more of him, and he said, "Here one has a very strong sense of history."

"That is what is wrong with Europe," Angelo said. "Too damn much history."

"It doesn't have to be a liability," Richard said, not meaning anything in particular, but trying to be polite, and hoping the conversation would veer away from him again. But Prince Vittorio said, "Pray continue."

"Well," Richard said, "I mean it depends on the history. If it's shameful, like—" He broke off in confusion; he had been about to say like Germany's, and he had only remembered in time that the Italians had been partners in the most shameful part of that era. They were all waiting for him now, and they knew why he had halted.

"Shameful like what, Mr. Delgard?" Vittorio said in English.

"Let us say," Richard looked squarely at the prince, "for example, shameful like our campaign against the Mexicans, or our earlier campaigns against the Indians, whom we 'liberated' against their wishes, and then 'protected' against fictitious enemies. Do you understand what I am trying to say?"

"Perfectly," said Vittorio, and there were pink spots on his cheeks. "In your history—"

"In our history," Richard interrupted, "there have been such shameful passages, but they are out of fashion now, and have been for a long time. Our past—"

"Your past," Angelo broke in, laughing. "You're like a virgin—you don't have enough past to put in your eye. All you've got is future. But us? We've got a past, and we can never forget it, because—how can we ever top it?"

Vittorio laughed, then, and explained to Diana. Angelo had saved the situation and Richard felt very grateful to him.

"He is a great thinker, the monster is," Massimo said, with genuine admiration. "Also he is very rich, and I will go to America next year and live in luxury at his expense."

"We will put you to work in the vineyards," Richard told him. "You will feel right at home."

"Will thee like that?" Massimo said to Ghita. "The monster says it is like Italy, but I do not believe it."

"If he says it," Ghita said, "it is true, I think."

"Yes," said Richard. "There is the sea, and the hills and the vineyards and the same hot sun. There is good wine, already approaching yours because there are many there who are Americans with the blood of Italy. There are many who, like my own grandparents, have kept the best of both places."

It was a long speech, and when he stopped, no one said anything for a moment. He looked at the tablecloth, thinking about home, and there was a sudden wrenching inside him, because he saw the San Mateo peninsula, and the ranch and the brown hills striated with the grapevines, and Burlingame and Pebble Beach, and that was where he had first raced against an enthusiastic novice named Charley Vollmer, who was now in an icebox in an Italian resort town six thousand miles from home. Everything seemed to cave in inside him, but he sat there like one of the immense statues in the salon upstairs, his face as forbidding and empty.

"You want to sit here all night?"

The dinner was over, and he was the only one still seated.

"I know you're not drunk," Angelo said.

"No," Richard said. He got up abruptly and the chair fell over with a clatter that made the nearby guests look around in amusement.

"But you're giving a good imitation."

"No," Richard said. "What happens now, dancing girls?"

"Are you sick?" Angelo asked with concern.

"No," Richard said, then, "yes, but not the way you mean."

Angelo shook his head. "Dancing upstairs. Put in an appearance and then go to bed. I need you sharp tomorrow."

"Yes," Richard said. *It went over and over in the air, the bright blue body glinting in the sun.* They walked across the open terrace and up the winding staircase to the salon, where the orchestra was playing very badly. Already the salon was full of dancing couples, and standing at the entrance, they watched Vittorio with Ghita, and Diana with Von Lutzow, but the German looked less sure of himself now, because he knew Diana was searching the crowd over his shoulder.

Angelo went away. Richard stood as if planted, and all the faces became a meaningless swirl. Now and then he was faintly aware of the music, but it only passed over the surface of his mind while he thought about the faded blue bundle of laundry on the hillside. I am getting near the end of it, he said to himself—I can feel that, although I don't know what the end will be like, only that something is rolling now, rolling faster and faster to a conclusion so final that there is certainly death in it somewhere, death of an idea or an ambition, but not for a change, defeat—not in any sense of the word. Ghita came to him. "Thee has not danced with me, Ricardo."

He made no move and she said, "There is no pleasure here for thee?"

He was unable to speak.

"Thee is crying?" she said in alarm. "Thy friend is dead."

He nodded, and tears spilled out of his eyes, but he stood there dumbly, making no move to brush them away. Ghita took his hand and led him outside and along the battlements to the circular platform atop one of the turrets. Another couple was there, embracing silently in the dark, but when Ghita and Richard came near, they broke apart and went hastily away.

The piazza looked far below and even the sound of the carnival seemed remote. Ghita crossed the turret and stood looking toward the sea, which glittered faintly under the waning moon. They did not speak for a long time, and then she said with finality: "But thee will race tomorrow."

"Yes."

She breathed deeply. "I will be glad when thee is home again, Ricardo."

"It will be soon."

"Thee speaks sweetly of the grandparents."

"They are my family."

"Thee has no mother or father?"

"My father was killed in an airplane crash many years ago. My mother decided she could not live without him."

She put her hand in his. "The old ones—I do not think they would like the English lady."

"If I loved her, they would love her," he said.

Thoughtfully, she said, "But thee does not love the English lady, Ricardo."

"No."

"That is good. Thee will find someone the grandparents can love for herself, not only because thee has chosen her."

"Perhaps."

"Thee doubts?"

He did not know how to answer. Everything was so inextricably mingled with the horror of Charley's crash that he was afraid to depend on his assessment of values, but the words she spoke seemed to ring with some meaning he could not grasp.

"That I will find one to love me as thee loves Massimo?" he said at last.

"No," she said. "Not like that. I have always loved Massimo. It is one of the earliest things I can remember, and so it will never change. But there are other kinds, Ricardo, no better, and no worse, but different. Man and woman—" she finished, as if it explained everything.

"I don't understand."

She looked around at him. "I have been badly educated—"

"It has nothing to do with education. Thee has a brain that is working better than mine—that's why I don't understand."

"But it is very simple," Ghita said. "It makes thee sad because thee loves me."

He felt as though he had been punched in the stomach. She stood so close to him, and it would be so easy to take her in his arms, and ruin everything. Desperate, he rammed his fists into his pockets.

"You knew that?"

"Massimo told me first. I did not believe him. But tonight I knew."

"Oh, my God," Richard said.

"That is why I have said I will be glad when thee has gone home again."

"I would never have said it, but I am glad it has been said."

"Yes," Ghita said. "I knew I would have to say it for

thee." For a moment she looked at him. "I must go back."

"I know."

"Good-bye, Ricardo." She held out her hand and he bent and kissed it formally.

"Good-bye." His throat ached with all the things unsaid as she went away from him through the shadows of the buttressed towers. Richard lighted a cigarette and waited, blowing the smoke into the fragrant night; when it was finished, he was about to flick the stub over the parapet into the ravine, but remembering in time, he ground it out underfoot instead.

It was necessary to fight his way through the mob in the piazza, and he reached the hotel with confetti in his hair, mouth and ears; he was smeared with lipstick and his white dinner jacket was forever ruined by the Chianti someone had slopped on his sleeve. The hotel itself was no haven. By the sounds, the tide of the carnival had already reached the bedrooms.

He could not find his key on the board, nor was there any sign of the clerk, so he went upstairs and along the corridor, trying to ignore the unmistakable sound-effects that came through the thin partitions. His own door was ajar, the key in the lock, and the light was on.

An old man lay on the bed, completely dressed, and dead drunk. He was small and very light and Richard grasped the lapels of the sodden jacket and lifted him with one hand like a sack of potatoes and laid him out gently in the corridor.

Nothing seemed to have been disturbed in the room, so Richard locked the door and undressed slowly, finding it difficult to work the coat sleeve off over the bandage. The hand was better now, he thought; Alciade had done a good job. But it was going to be hard to write with it.

He pulled down the window shade to shut out the sight of the piazza and sat down at the little table.

How do you start such a letter, he wondered, when you don't know anything at all about the people you're addressing—or whether they exist at all.

He wrote:

To Charley's family,
     I did not know Charley very well, having met him only once before at Pebble Beach, but we were friends, and I was with him when he died.

I am writing you because I believe you would want to know he was not alone at the end, and that he did not suffer. Mercifully, he never came out of the coma. On the chance that he might have been Catholic, last rites were performed and absolution granted.

Perhaps—and I fervently hope it—there will be some measure of consolation for you, as there is for me, in the knowledge that Charley died to save the life of a child. I saw it happen. No one could have blamed him had he chosen instead to stay on the road, and in so doing, injure the youngster. In fact, it took almost a superhuman effort to leave the course in time to avoid running over the child. He did not hesitate, and surely he knew the penalty. That is heroism, I think, in the truest sense of the word.

It had taken Richard a long time to write it, and now, reading it over, he was not satisfied with it, but he did not know how to improve it. Several times during the war he had had to write letters like it, but at least there was the solace of a collective national sorrow for the parents, and the salve of patriotic pride.

He would be in Rome in a few days, and by then the embassy would have traced Charley's relatives; he sealed the letter in an envelope, on which he wrote: Please forward to the family of Charles Vollmer of California, American citizen, who died in San Gregorio, Italy, September 23rd.

It was midnight when he went to bed.

He awoke later, disturbed by the sound of angry voices. Turning over, he buried his face in the pillow, trying to drift back into unconsciousness. One of the voices was Massimo's, and for a moment Richard lay still, until he could orient himself. Instantly, he was wide awake. The carnival was over for the night, with only an occasional distant voice raised in drunken song, and the piazza was silent but for Massimo's low, deadly tones.

Richard went to the window. Massimo was standing in front of the hotel in the gloom, holding something in his hand as he looked at another window, beyond Richard's window.

"Come out, you pig, you dog, come out—" he was saying over and over.

Then the other voice, in broken Italian: "Don't be a damned fool! Who are you to complain?" It was Von

Lutzow's voice, and Richard's heart began to pound with dread.

"Come out, you swine," Massimo said, "and I will show you who I am to complain."

"I won't fight you," Von Lutzow said contemptuously. "You're not big enough to fight your own battles, and I don't intend to take on the whole village."

"Come out, filth. No one else will touch you—I would kill anyone who tried. I am big enough for you!"

"Go sleep it off," Von Lutzow said in a tone of dismissal. "You took my girl, I took yours. It means nothing—"

And then Massimo called him something. It was what the Italian mobs had screamed at the retreating Nazis as they fought desperately back up the peninsula in the face of the advancing Allied armies, and it was so unspeakably vile that to say it was to invite death from anyone who could strike back. Silence for a moment, then Richard heard Von Lutzow's hoarse whisper:

"I am coming—"

Massimo retreated a few steps and braced himself, and now Richard could see what he held in his hand—the buggy whips.

Von Lutzow's feet went along the silent corridor while Richard was struggling into pants and sweater and moccasins. He ran down the hall, took the stairway in two jumps and came out into the piazza.

No one spoke. Massimo stood waiting as Von Lutzow advanced. As soon as the German was in range, Massimo lashed at him, and the sound of the thongs hitting Von Lutzow's face was loud in the echoing square. Hans rushed him, taking two more strokes of the whip in order to get his hands on Massimo.

He hit Massimo on the cheek, and in the side, and then Richard was on them. They were fighting like animals, and Richard had to use all his power to rip them apart and hold them, and then the German ducked under Richard's hand, boring in at Massimo. Richard caught him by the collar as he passed, jerked him upright, and hit him with the back of his hand.

The blow lifted Von Lutzow off his feet and spun him around and dropped him on his face on the cobbles. He didn't move. Massimo swung his body and aimed a kick at the German's head, but Richard yanked him sideways.

"That's enough," Richard said. "That's enough, Massimo."

But Massimo looked insane with rage. He continued his impersonal struggle to free himself from Richard, and it was perfectly clear that he intended to kill his fallen enemy.

Suddenly it was over. Massimo went limp. Richard barely caught him before he fell, and the cobblestones were black with blood in the darkness.

Richard sat smoking on the roof of Ghita's house, watching the clumps of people below in the piazza, the people on the hillside steps, and the people going and coming from the church, which was open, although it was after three in the morning, because the village had heard that Massimo was dying.

Doctor Alciade was in the room beneath with the two doctors of the race committee, and Ghita and Angelo and Uncle Fausto and the priest, Don Ludovico. The doctors had done what little they could for the body, and now the priest was preparing the soul.

Rubbing his face wearily, Doctor Alciade came onto the roof. "You have another cigarette?"

Richard gave him one and they smoked in silence, until Uncle Fausto appeared, looking in dumb appeal to the doctor, who said, almost angrily, "He's dead already—he just doesn't know it." Uncle Fausto went into the corner of the roof and stood looking at the stars.

"What the devil happened?" Alciade asked.

"I don't know," Richard said. He knew part of it, but that wasn't the part the doctor was curious about. After a while Angelo came up, and Richard said, "Will the race be canceled?"

"Why should it be?" Angelo said in surprise.

"The race must go on," Richard said.

"What?"

"Nothing."

One of the race committee doctors came up then with Felice and Giorgio. Felice looked at Angelo, the tears running down his face. "I gave him my blood, but it didn't help. I would have given him every drop, but—" He shut his mouth and tried to stop the sobs. His brother put his arms around him and held him close.

"Take him home," Angelo said. "Give him a sleeping

pill. He has to drive in a few hours." Giorgio nodded and led his brother off the roof.

Mechanically Richard said, "He's shot. He won't drive."

"How are you?" said Angelo.

"All right."

"You'd better go home, too."

"No."

"There's nothing you can do here."

"No," Richard said again, not moving, and Angelo did not argue. Alciade went over to speak to the other doctor, and Angelo said, "You saw it?"

"I was in it," Richard said grimly.

"I thought it was all finished when Hans left the castle. I didn't think he would start anything again."

"He didn't," Richard said. "I don't know what happened at the castle, but the first thing I knew, Massimo was calling Hans out of the hotel. He was pretty rough. So Hans went out and Massimo whipped him, and then I got there."

"What do you mean—whipped?"

"With whips. They were only toys, but they can hurt."

"You stopped it?"

"But not in time. He'd already slugged Massimo pretty hard. Hard enough, I guess."

Angelo said, "The race committee wants to know what happened. Nobody seems to know, but they all suspect something. They're wondering whether to bar Hans from the race."

Richard said, "It would be a good idea to shut up about it, Angelo."

"You think so?"

"Yes. If the word gets around, Hans will wind up facing a manslaughter charge—if he's lucky. If the village finds out, they'll probably lynch him."

"Nobody saw the fight?"

"I don't think so." He thought of something else. "Who knows what started it?"

Angelo said, "I do. Prince Vittorio, Diana, Massimo, Hans, Ghita, maybe Geoffrey—who can guess what he knows? Probably some of the castle servants—they always know—but they won't talk."

"I still don't know."

"You can guess. Massimo sneaked off somewhere with Diana for a long time. Hans was furious. He got Ghita alone outside, and apparently he thought she was being coy when she said no. Massimo found out about it. Period."

"I thought I'd broken his neck. I wish I had."

"It isn't broken, but it will be stiff for a long time. Be careful of him."

"Let him stay away from me," Richard said.

The third doctor came up on the roof. "Is there somebody here named Ricardo?"

Richard went down the steps into the house. Only Ghita and the priest were with Massimo now. He lay propped up in bed in a clean nightshirt and his eyes were closed and his face looked blue against the pillows. They were airing the room and the candle flames danced in the dawn breeze; the room was so full of candles it looked like a chapel.

In a whisper, Richard said, "You sent for me?"

Ghita looked at the bed. "He wants you."

The doctor came back in now. He said, "Don't make him talk."

"What is the difference," Massimo said with his eyes still closed, "if I am to die anyway? Get out, Doctor. You too, Father. I have things to say to these others."

"I forbid you to talk, Massimo—"

"Get out," Massimo said. "I make my own rules now. Get out."

"My son," began Don Ludovico, but Massimo opened his eyes and said, "You have both given me up; your responsibility is finished. I am on my own. Get out."

They went. Massimo's eyes danced and he looked excited. "Sit close, so I will not have to yell."

Ghita put two chairs close beside the bed.

"Take my hand," Massimo said. It was a grubby, child's hand that he held out. Ghita lay her hand on his palm, and Richard enfolded both in his own. "Thee remembers telling me of the bad feeling?"

"Yes."

"Thee said this was the moment of the big risk, and that only an idiot is not afraid."

"Something like that."

"I have known the feeling," Massimo said, smiling, "and I was not afraid."

"Then thee must be an idiot," Richard said.

"Yes," Massimo said. "A lion of an idiot."

There was no strength and no warmth in the hand they held, but there was both in Ghita's hand.

"They say this idiot is going to die," Massimo whispered. "Which shows who the real idiots are. I cannot die now. There are too many things to do. I refuse to die."

"Then thee won't," Richard said.

"Of course not." His eyes went to Ghita. "I love thee greatly."

"Hush," she said.

"But I have not been good for thee."

"Hush," she said. "I love thee, and it is enough."

"No," he said. "Nothing is ever enough. It is the only word in the language that makes me angry."

"I have what I want," Ghita said, soothing him.

"Does thee know, Ricardo," Massimo said, "that this ignorant peasant girl is the wisest and best of women?"

"Hush, foolish one," Ghita said.

"Don't hush me. These are things to be said in case I have made a mistake and they are right. Answer me, monster."

"Yes."

"And thee loves her wholly?"

Richard swallowed. "Yes."

"And if they are right, thee will care for her, as I would —better than I would?"

"Please, Massimo—" Ghita began, but he interrupted her.

"Quiet, woman. Answer me, monster."

"If you both wish it," Richard said.

"I wish it," Massimo said. "I wish that thee will take her home with thee. There will be nothing here for her afterward."

"Stop it, Massimo," Ghita said, her face wet.

"But thee is rich, and can give her a home, and educate her—if thee wants an educated wife—and even teach her English, and have many babies—" He turned his head away. "Is it truly like this where you live? Truly?"

"Much," Richard said. "Not the village. But the sea, and the hills, and the vineyards. Even the same flowers."

"And olive trees?"

"And olive trees. But not very good ones yet."

"They can grow anything there," Massimo said to Ghita. "Thee will go with him."

"If you both wish me to," she said.

Richard nodded.

"Then it is a promise, Ricardo, and I trust thee." He relaxed against the pillow with his eyes closed for a moment. Then he opened them and said in his normal voice, "Now get out, monster, so I can get some sleep. Otherwise I will drive badly this afternoon."

"It's a good idea," Richard said, but his face showed that he was only humoring Massimo, who said, "Weren't thee paying attention? I said they are wrong."

Richard said, "Sleep well, my friend. Good night."

He withdrew his hand, and went out of the house.

Chapter Thirteen

A NGELO came into Richard's bedroom at eleven in the morning, looking like a man who has seen everything.

"Well?" Richard said.

"I've just witnessed the second resurrection," Angelo said. "He's not only alive, he's up. He's not only up, he's going to drive."

"You're crazy."

"*I'm crazy?*"

"But he can't possibly have the strength," Richard said angrily. "You mustn't let him! The scar will open up and he'll hemorrhage again—he could kill twenty people if he passed out at the wheel."

"Do you want to sit on him?" Angelo said. "Or maybe we could buy a nice straitjacket?"

"Don't be a jerk," Richard said. "If the doctors won't certify him, the race committee won't let him drive. That's all there is to it."

Angelo laughed shortly. "There are more things in heaven and earth, Ricardo, than are dreamed of in your philosophy."

"Screw the mysticism, Angelo," Richard said heavily. He put his feet on the floor. "Pass me those cigarettes. What did the doctors say?"

"They said he can drive."

"Some doctors!"

Angelo looked faintly amused. "I keep forgetting that you're not really Italian, Ricardo."

"Bear it in mind," Richard said rudely. He was disgusted with Massimo most of all; never having himself been capable of the grandstand play he was acutely embarrassed when he recognized it in others, and he thought of this as a kind of mock heroism, counterfeiting what Charley Vollmer had done.

When Angelo had gone, he bathed, scrubbing almost as carefully as a doctor preparing for an operation. Then he put on a new pair of white coveralls and went downstairs to breakfast. The tension was heavy in his stomach by now, and he was all through worrying about anybody else. He was the only man in the world who was about to drive a racing car.

139

Richard took as long over breakfast as he could, drinking two pots of coffee afterward, and it was still only one o'clock. It would have been good to take a walk, but there seemed to be a million people milling around in the piazza, and he did not want to see or talk to anyone. While he was eating, he had heard the church bells, and he knew there was a special Mass for the drivers; ordinarily, he would have gone with the others, but he did not feel like one of them today. He felt like the man on the high diving board who wonders how he got there.

The strong bitter coffee had left his mouth dry, so he went upstairs and brushed his teeth and drank three glasses of water, remembered to take a package of chewing gum, and went downstairs and pushed his way through the crowds toward the Scuderia Barzio pit.

Already thousands had found their places along the course as far as he could see in both directions. Except for the clear lane between the pits and the grandstand, the square was solid with people, and every window overlooking it sprouted a dozen heads. But the grandstand itself was reserved for persons of importance, and so it was only sparsely populated this early; no one had appeared in what looked like the royal box.

He passed the back of the GRP pit and saw Geoffrey busy with his two mechanics; they were in frantic haste, apparently just completing the installation of the spare engine. Geoffrey looked up and they nodded, and Richard went on to the rear of his own pit.

Massimo was not there, but all the others were, including Angelo's personal timekeepers. Everyone spoke a curt good morning and went on trying to look busy. Richard found his goggles and began polishing them.

"What about the rain Uncle Fausto promised us?"

Giorgio was carefully cleaning his tools, one by one, and laying them out neatly in formation on the pit counter. "If it is going to rain, it will rain."

"I'm relieved to know," Richard said.

Giorgio smiled at him. "It is a good day."

"It is very hot."

"But not too hot."

"No. Not too hot."

"As long as it is not too hot, there may not be rain, although, of course, there could be."

"I agree, without reservation," Richard said, and they

grinned thinly at each other. He went over and sat on
the pit counter beside Felice, who put an affectionate
hand on his shoulder, but only for a moment, and very
lightly.

"All goes well with thee?" Richard said.

"Well enough." Felice seemed calm. "And for thee?"

"Well, also, thank you."

"It is a good day."

"Yes, it is fine."

"Only that the machines go well."

"Yes." They sat watching the activity at the other pits,
and then Angelo asked Richard to try Number Three for
size, because they had cut back the cowling a little to re-
locate the seat farther to the rear for him.

Richard inserted himself into the still cramped cockpit, trying to make it look roomy. "It is very much better,"
he said, and it was true that he could reach the pedals
with less acrobatics.

"You see, I worry about your comfort," Angelo said.
"Because I expect you to win."

Richard looked up at him. "It could happen."

"No one has a better chance." No one was thinking
seriously about Massimo.

"Felice seems all right."

"I'm not betting on him." For a moment Angelo waited,
quiet in the bright sun, listening to the noise of the crowd.
"I have much faith in thee, Ricardo."

"Truly?" he answered with polite cynicism. Angelo
usually preferred to speak English with Richard, unless
he was being sarcastic, or wanted something, and now
that he had switched to Italian, Richard braced himself.

"If thee shows up as well as I know thee can," Angelo
said casually, "thee can be Number One for the Scuderia
Barzio next season."

This is why he wanted me to sit in the car, Richard
told himself; it's Angelo's idea of salesmanship. It should
work—it should make me go out there and do or die for
old Winsocki. "Hit that line," Richard said aloud in a
stern voice; "block that kick, we wanna touchdown, yik-
yik-yik!" He laughed. He was earning his letter, and he
would have to buy a handknit sweater with the initials
SB, and tell everyone it stood for Southern Balifornia.
It had come too late, or too early; he only knew that the
race itself was too big in his mind and stomach to need

any additional weight of inducement in the form of future rewards.

The race committee was in the timing stand now and the band was playing valiantly. A parade of *carabinieri* appeared, broke formation, and began shooing the usual horde of people with various official armbands back toward the pits and the stands, to clear the starting grid; scores of photographers—press and amateur—protested their right to remain, but the police shoved them anyway. A whistle blew and the drivers began strolling toward the timing booth to be addressed by the chief steward of the course.

"Let's go, Felice." Richard got out of Number Three and started across the cobbles. Already the racing machines were being pushed into position on the grid.

The drivers stood around in a self-conscious circle, hands on hips, or fingering their goggles and gloves. A few of them tried to joke, but it was not successful. Each man was too full of himself to have room for any other. Geoffrey and Von Lutzow joined the other side of the circle and Richard noticed that the German held his head a little awkwardly, and there were marks on his cheekbone.

Above them in the timing booth a heated discussion was going on, but then the chief steward said something final and he and the starter came down the ladder.

"Well, gentlemen, are we all here?"

Nobody answered him, nor did he expect them to. "I presume you are familiar with the regulations, with the exception of one change. It has been decided to permit overtaking in the chute—I am assured there is no excessive risk. But no passing on the bridge—"

There was a burst of nervous laughter from the drivers at this absurdity, but the chief steward went on, "No passing between the castle turn and the water splash. Anywhere else, it is permitted. Flags: green—clear course; orange—slow down, maintaining your relative positions; red—stop immediately wherever you are; blue and yellow —watch out for oil on the course just beyond the flag marshal; black—you are ordered into your pit, and that's an order, gentlemen. But I trust it won't be necessary to black-flag anyone. I know most of you, and I know you for sportsmen. Remember that not only courtesy but safety requires that you give way to a car that is capable of overtaking you. I will not permit deliberate balking. Any questions?"

If there were, they were engulfed by the sudden, deafening roar of the crowd. The drivers flinched nervously and looked up at the stands. The spectators were on their feet, shrieking with excitement. Richard turned.

Far across the square, and high on the hillside stairway, was a small figure in white coveralls, descending slowly, but unassisted . . . and the whole world seemed to be waiting for him. He moved unhurriedly, and Richard knew that he was making an effort, and a great wave of pity flooded through him, dissolving his earlier resentment, and leaving in its wake a kind of awe at such dogged single-mindedness. He began to perceive in how basic a fashion he and Massimo differed: the truth was that Massimo had never been, and could not be, defeated; the philosophy of retiring to lick one's wounds and living to fight another day was the product of a far more sophisticated world than Massimo's. He would never stop fighting. He could be cheated by bad luck, overpowered, or killed; but he could not be defeated, for defeat exists only in the acceptance of it.

The crowd was wild with joy for Massimo, the victor; what was to come could not change it in any way. In their minds, this was the triumph. They parted for him as he came across the piazza; they screamed his name and waved their arms and jostled around him. But no one touched him, any more than they would have touched Caesar.

Massimo came directly to Number One, which was waiting with the other racing machines on the starting grid. He had the pole position, with one of the new hush-hush Maseratis on his right, and then Richard's Number Three Ferrari beyond. The second six-cylinder Maserati was directly behind Massimo, with Von Lutzow in the GRP next, and Felice just behind Richard. Geoffrey had the other GRP with the untried engine in the third row, which he shared with the remaining Gordini and the older, four-cylinder Maserati. Behind them were four more rows of three, but there was nothing to fear among them. The winner, barring acts of God, was somewhere in the first three rows.

The whole Barzio team stood around Number One as Massimo buckled his seat belt.

"How do you feel, runt?" Richard said.

"Fine," Massimo said, "sitting down."

"Remember," Angelo said flatly, "if you begin to feel bad, you'll pull up immediately."

"I'm not crazy," Massimo said.

"You can't prove it," Richard said.

Massimo took a surgical mask out of his pocket and tied it over his nose and mouth; it would help to keep some of the irritating dust and smoke fumes out of his throat. The chief steward and the starter came over and patted Massimo on the shoulder, but they did not look happy. Angelo said, "You don't have to worry. He promised."

"I do have to worry," the chief steward said. "Remember it's seventy laps. Save yourself as much as you can." He walked away.

"All right," Angelo said. "Like I said. I want Felice out in front as soon as possible. Run those new Maseratis to death—can you do it?" Felice jerked his head. Angelo went on, "Ricardo will run interference for Massimo at the head of the pack. You won't need to refuel, only oil and water. I figure two tire changes, and I'll be the judge of when. By thirty laps things should be pretty well sorted out."

Richard said, "Be ready to come through, Felice. I'll pull wide on the flag."

Felice nodded, his lips pressed together.

"Be careful of Hans," Angelo said softly. "That's all."

The loudspeaker blared: "Start engines!"

Richard ran around the tail of the Maserati and climbed into the Ferrari, turning on the switch as he settled in the seat. They were not using the portable electric starters, so the two mechanics drew the car back a few feet and then shoved it forward. Richard let in the clutch and the engine screamed into life; he brought the car to a halt with the front tires on the stripe of white paint, and looked across at Amadeo in the Maserati and beyond him to Massimo. Giorgio and Angelo were just push-starting Number One, and behind Richard, the mechanics were doing the same for Felice.

Richard shoved the cotton plugs into his ears and pulled his helmet down tight and buckled it; for the first time he forgot to touch the dent for good luck. He settled the goggles over his eyes and wondered again if it would rain.

Automatically, his foot kept up an intermittent blipping of the throttle to keep the plugs from oiling up. The glove was too tight over his bandaged hand, and he thought it might stop the circulation; he tried to decide whether there was time to signal the pit for a knife to cut the seam open. But the flag was up, and all of the twenty-one unmuffled engines opened up in a crescendo of sonic blasts that ripped the air apart and hammered painfully on ears and faces. Richard opened his mouth and yelled to equalize the pressure, without being able to hear his own voice.

The starter was looking toward the stands, and Richard threw a glance that way and saw Prince Vittorio, standing, Ghita beside him in crown and costume, and the handkerchief was just drifting from His Highness's fingers— Richard let in the clutch, and he was moving even as the starter's flag swept downward.

He was first off the line, with Massimo only a fraction behind. Richard pulled wide to the right, going down toward the left-hand turn at the castle corner, but the car that came through the gap was Von Lutzow's, with Felice on his tail, shouting and waving a furious fist. The German bore to the left, and Massimo in the Maserati had to ease off to avoid a collision; the order into the turn was Von Lutzow, Felice, Amadeo in the Maserati, and then Richard and Massimo. They went through the lower town in that order, and they were so close together they looked like a train.

Now that they were under way, Richard relaxed, and waited for the remembered enjoyment to begin. Hans led the parade through the narrow streets, and he was driving admirably; already it seemed certain that he intended to go all out, all the way. Richard knew he would be a hard man to overtake, except perhaps on the straights.

They went across the water splash like a serpent, and shot up the side of the mountain. Both Felice and the Maserati tried now, but Von Lutzow found something extra and maintained his lead. The order was unchanged as they went through the curve at the top of the climb, although the Maserati overdid it, and caromed off the straw bales placed to prevent cars from sliding against the mountainside. Amadeo corrected, and saved his third position, but it was necessary for Richard to take violent evasive action, and in doing so, he lost revs and speed.

Already the GRP and Number Two Ferrari were well out on the Mountain Straight, pulling away fast; then, after a considerable gap, the Maserati, accelerating like the wind, another gap, and then Richard and Massimo.

Far ahead, he caught a glimpse of the leaders. Felice had pulled out abreast of Von Lutzow, but he did not really want to pass him, only to chivvy the German into going faster and faster. At the distant hairpin, Felice yielded, and went around it so close behind Hans they looked tied together. But that was their private race, not Richard's. His race was only with the car just in front— the Maserati, and the other nineteen cars might not have been in the race at all. His job was to keep the Maserati within striking distance, without blowing himself up in the attempt. Deciding on a fifty-yard interval, he found he could maintain it along the Mountain Straight without exceeding seventy-five hundred revs, but he wished he knew whether the Maserati had anything in reserve.

Richard led Massimo neatly through the hairpin, and out of the corner of his eye he spotted Felice already slamming over the bridge in pursuit of Von Lutzow. Now sweeping back along the mountainside toward the head of the chute, the memory of Charley flashed through his mind, but he put it away from him, trying not to see where the wheel tracks in the grass led off into nothing. He turned down into the chute, screeching through the S-bend, and bounced over the bridge; the Ferrari boosted itself away from the building and turned down toward the piazza, tires smoking under the fierce acceleration.

As he passed the pits, the crowds in the stands rose, but not for him, he knew. They were urging Massimo on, wanting to see him in the lead. Angelo stood well out on the track, holding up both hands with finger and thumb together. He wanted them to continue just as they were. Richard wondered what the lap time had been, guessing it to be several seconds slower than practice—probably about two minutes, ten seconds. Next time around they would have the board out with the lap time chalked on it.

The second of the six-cylinder Maseratis passed him at the water splash, and took a warning shake of the fist from the flag marshal for doing so. Richard maintained his pace, and saw with satisfaction that Geoffrey was trying unsuccessfully to overtake on the climb; the GRP had to drop back just behind Massimo for the left-hander at the top, and they negotiated that turn without change of position. But as soon as they were on the straight, Geoffrey pulled out and made another bid. Richard added throttle, and they raced side by side for half a mile before the Ferrari reached its maximum. Geoffrey pulled back in line, and a blue car came through like a streak of light, passing all three of them, and barely slowing down enough for the hairpin. It was the Gordini, and Varenne knew how to make it go.

Passing the pits again, Richard read the board held by Giorgio: 6th—2.9. It meant he held sixth position and the time was about what he expected. Angelo's doubled fists meant that he was to hold that position, even if it meant opening up to do so.

It meant just that. Geoffrey tried once more on the climb, with the older Maserati on his tail. They came up on the inside of the two Ferraris, and all four cars went into the top turn in a tight bunch. This time Richard let the revs go all the way up, but again they were halfway along the straight before he could shake Geoffrey off.

Richard was too fast in the hairpin, and slid wildly, and Massimo had to pass him or run into him; he passed, and Geoffrey got through too. Richard corrected, swearing violently, and roared off after them, his stomach still fluttering. In the chute he really bore down. Massimo stayed well over, seeing him coming, and he shot past both of them; he would have liked to signal his thanks to Massimo, but already the bridge was upon him and he had more speed than ever before. He went into the drift, leaped into the air—and knew a moment of absolute terror because it looked as if he would hurtle straight into the building without even getting his wheels on the ground. The Ferrari landed with a sickening jolt that should have broken his back, or the car's, and skidded against the straw bales along the base of the building. The bales bounced him, spinning, back onto the road, and miraculously headed properly down into the piazza.

He looked back at his right rear wheel as he crossed the square. It looked all right, but he was trailing a plume of straw and there was a large dent in the tail, so he prayed fervently that the fuel tank was not cracked.

He was angry and disgusted as he began the third lap. Already he had made two bad mistakes in judgment in a business where even one is often too many. Settle down, baby, he told himself, and live longer—a little less horse-power and a little more brains.

After that he' began to find his form. Geoffrey contin-ued to challenge, on curves and on the straights, and Rich-ard simply outdrove him, cornering always just under the limit, placing the red machine always on the exact line, and depending on the Ferrari's acceleration and slightly superior top speed to stave off the GRP bids on the straights. Already there were casualties. Three cars were being worked on at the pits; the old Maserati had over-shot at the bridge, hit the building and been pushed out of the way by the crowd, its driver disconsolately survey-ing the wreckage as Richard came through. One of the overhead-cam Veritas streamliners had been abandoned on the Mountain Straight. The next time around he saw a' car upside down with one wheel missing, lying against the side of the hotel, and the ambulance moving through the crowd. He couldn't identify the car, but he knew it was not one of the leaders.

Lap 12, said the board, to Richard's surprise. He thought he had done more. Massimo was still just behind him, and now they were lapping the stragglers, but they themselves had not been lapped by Von Lutzow or any of the other leaders.

The second of the six-cylinder Maseratis was at the pits on the fifteenth lap, and after another round the Gor-dini was in also, having its plugs changed. The board said:

LAP 16

VON
FEL .
AMA
38 SEC

So Von Lutzow was still leading, Felice was second, and Amadeo's Maserati third—thirty-eight seconds ahead of Richard, who was in fourth place by virtue of other people's mechanical troubles.

The Ferrari was still going perfectly, his fears about a split tank apparently having been groundless. But the rear tires—especially the right one—were completely bald. He hoped Angelo would bring him in for the tire change soon; the idea of one of those weakened casings blowing

out on the bridge made his stomach tighten. He realized
he also wanted badly to split his glove open—his fingers
were so stiff he could barely uncurl them from the wheel.

Angelo brought him in on the twentieth lap. He remembered to brake in time to avoid overshooting the pit,
and the car was barely stopped before they had it up on
the jacks and were hammering at the wheel nuts. Angelo
handed him a bottle of water and a clean rag and knelt
with Giorgio to examine the rear axle. Richard took a
gulp, washed out his mouth, and then drank a little,
handed back the bottle and began wiping his dusty goggles.

"Gimme a knife," he yelled. The two rear wheels were
already changed, and now the mechanics were putting in
oil and water.

"No visible damage," Angelo said. "It goes well?"

"Yes," Richard said. "For Christ's sake, where's that
knife?"

"Coming," Giorgio said.

"Same orders?" Richard said. "Here—cut it down the
seam, it's too tight."

"You're averaging two-nine. I want you to step it up
three seconds per lap. You're a minute behind Felice now,
but I'm bringing him in on the twenty-fifth."

"Hans will need tires soon, too—"

"Yes—get going!" He was down off the jacks, the
switch was on, and they were pushing him. The engine
caught and he moved out into the roadway, letting two
other cars pass, and accelerated for the castle corner.

He calculated that he had been in the pits for about
half a minute, so Von Lutzow and Felice should be close
behind him, Massimo and Geoffrey were probably just
reaching the Mountain Straight. Beyond that he no longer
had any clear picture of the situation. From now on he
would have to race strictly according to pit signals, because he would only know what they chose to tell him.

Pick up three seconds per lap? He didn't need a stop
watch for that. It was a thing you knew from experience,
and it meant going a little deeper into the corners, braking
a little harder, and drifting closer to the limits of adhesion.

The blood was coming back into his hand now, and it
hurt like hell, but the fingers were less stiff. On the climb
he passed the Veritas and the HWM that had gone by
as he was leaving the pit. At the entrance to the Mountain Straight, he came on Geoffrey's car facing in the

wrong direction, but there was room .to get by and they waved at each other. He could just see Massimo going over the bridge far below.

This is monotonous, Richard told himself. He passed one car after another with no particular difficulty, but they were all cars which had gone by during his pit stop.

Going through the square again, he saw Massimo pouring water over his bare head, while Number One got new tires; from what little Richard could see while passing the pit area at a hundred miles an hour, Massimo looked all right, and they had not even lifted the hood of his machine.

The Gordini and both new Maseratis were back in the race now, which only complicated the order of things; and then both Felice and Von Lutzow were in for tires, too. The next time around, they were gone, and the board said:

LAP 26

RIC
GEOFF
MASS

He couldn't figure that out, unless both the German and Felice had lost an awful lot of time during their stops, and were perhaps half a lap behind him. Well, it wasn't his problem, he was only running against time.

The board informed him that he was averaging two-six now, equal to his best practice time, but it didn't seem very fast any more because he knew the course so exactly that it had become almost automatic. He went around and around, and he was still leading, because the board said so, and it was a pleasant sensation, although he had no illusions about it—the race was only half over.

On the thirty-eighth lap there was a bad crash in the chute. Richard saw the smoke as he came onto the Mountain Straight, but at this .distance he had no idea what had happened. At the head of the chute, the marshal was waving the orange flag, so he slowed down and drove at a sedate pace through the S-bend. From the tire marks, it appeared that one machine had rammed another while braking for the bridge. They had gone off on opposite sides of the road, the one breaking in half around a tree, the other lying on its side in the ditch, blazing furiously.

One of the drivers looked unhurt, but the other was standing dumbly looking at a couple of First Aid men; he was leaning forward and both arms dangled awkwardly.

In his concern, Richard forgot to keep the engine revving up, so that when he remembered, and down-shifted and opened the throttle, the engine backfired and vibrated violently. He crossed the bridge in a series of jerks, holding the throttle open in second gear, until the fouled plugs in one cylinder cleared themselves and the cylinder went to work again, but the fourth cylinder was still dead. Hoping it would clear, he decided not to stop at the pit. Going downhill across the square and through the lower town, he was hitting on all four again, but the engine began to miss badly on the uphill climb. At the top he had only two cylinders.

Nursing the engine, he turned onto the straight, not pressing at all, and after a few moments one cylinder came back, but the other one showed no sign of life. He looked behind him.

Massimo was close behind him once more, but Geoffrey was coming up fast with Von Lutzow and Amadeo getting ready to pass him. Richard waved Massimo on, and Number One fled past, Massimo looking strangely top-heavy under the helmet and goggles and mask. The others passed Richard before he got to the bridge. He arrived at the pit, pointing at the engine.

"Plugs!" he yelled.

They had the hood off. He got water for himself and for the engine; he got oil and a new set of plugs, and—as long as he was here—a new set of rear tires. But he knew he had lost a good half-lap for his carelessness.

Three stupidities; he could not afford any more. It did not require a mathematician to tell him that he was about a minute behind the leaders, with thirty laps to go. To catch them he would have to pick up another two seconds per lap, going around in two minutes four seconds, two seconds faster than his best previous time, and equal to the best time Massimo had put up in practice. And for thirty laps. Impossible.

He felt very tired, and he suddenly realized how cramped his legs were; his hand felt raw and he supposed it had opened up again. There was no point in trying any harder than he had been, because he had neither the strength nor the ability to lap this course for another hour at two-four. Angelo was crazy to think he could do it, Richard thought with vague anger. The smart thing was to keep on lapping at two-six and be ready when and if the leaders found they couldn't stand the pace either. That was the smart thing. And if they all keep running like clockwork, and don't make any mistakes, you'll finish sixth or seventh, which is no disgrace, and with the consolation that you've driven a good race, driven it fairly intelligently, and to the best of your ability. But there did not seem to be much consolation in the thought.

What is a consolation prize? he asked himself, and answered: A prize -you accept for being defeated. That god-damned district attorney. You're a great fellow for figuring other people out—people like Massimo—but you haven't been able to figure out what's lacking in you. What the hell difference does it make whether you actually cross the line first, so long as you don't accept the defeat in advance? That's all very well for Massimo, he's got the talent to justify that kind of driving. Alibis, you lawyer, you. What is Massimo? A half-dead half-pint—and what do you think he's using for strength about now? Nothing that you'd even know the name of, Delgard; when you've got it, you don't need anything else.

He did not make any decision. But there was a slow anger that he felt through his bones, and now instead of being weighted with fatigue, he had a pleasant sense of relaxed weariness, allied with a co-ordination that seemed to have another dimension. Without trying any harder than before, he found himself driving faster, and he began to perceive dimly what that other dimension might be. It was more than the exultant sense of doing something perfectly—it was a kind of magic, a spirit that flowed into all the channels of the mind and body; the magic touched even the machine, flowing through the fingertips, so that it was not even like driving now, it was like flying, and it was like a song. The magic did not tell you that you would win anything, but with it you knew that you could.

Richard had never held the wheel so lightly, nor paced a racing machine with such delicacy; he was driving by instinct, and the board that Angelo held wasn't needed to tell him what he already knew.

On lap sixty he had the leaders in sight as he climbed the mountainside; they were still far ahead, already going through the hairpin, but at least he was not racing alone any more. He caught and passed a slowing Felice in the chute. Number Two sounded rough and its driver looked exhausted. Overtaking, Richard kissed his gloved fingertips to Felice, who replied with a wan smile.

The board showed that Massimo was leading, with Amadeo's Maserati second and Von Lutzow third, while Geoffrey was still swapping fourth place with the Gordini. The next time around, the German had moved into the lead. The leaders were running together, passing and repassing, and after a forty-yard interval, Geoffrey and the Gordini having a private scrap, the green GRP faster through the curves and the lower town, the blue French car making it up on the straights. And always the red Number Three Ferrari moved up.

On the sixty-fifth, Richard began to sense something wrong with his rear suspension. The complete accord with the machine was lost; in the corners it was unpredictable and almost malevolent; it behaved like a skittish horse that shies at its own shadow, and Richard knew he should slow down before the car broke up under him, but he had no intention of doing so. He could win now, and as long as the machine could stay on the road, he would keep on pushing it.

Climbing beyond the water splash, he inched up on the Gordini, using the full eight thousand revs; the engine had been babied for the first half of the race, and now it would have to begin putting out. He passed the Gordini and went into the top turn level with the rear wheels of the GRP. The rear end of the Ferrari skittered dangerously, but he corrected automatically, expecting it, without losing more than a length, and then they were roaring along the straight, fullbore, side by side, with the Gordini on his tail, waiting for room to use his superior speed.

Richard used most of the Mountain Straight getting past Geoffrey, and the Frenchman came through the gap behind him. The hairpin was negotiated with no margin of safety at all, and then they were approaching the chute, and turning down into it, and both Geoffrey and the Gordini were attempting to repass. Richard got to the bridge first, and fastest, and went over it in a way that couldn't have done the failing suspension any good, and then slammed down into the piazza.

His heart nearly stopped, because Massimo was at the pit—but he had apparently only gone in for a drink of water, because they were already pushing him away as he passed the water bottle back. Richard went by him like the wind and dove down into the lower town, on fire with impatience to catch the leaders. He knew that if Massimo had sacrificed precious seconds this late in the race, he must have had no choice, and now it was up to Richard.

By this time, the right rear shock absorber was nearly useless, but as long as the axle stayed in place, he would keep on racing. He came into the piazza the sixty-seventh time only ten feet behind Amadeo's Maserati, with Von Lutzow barely a car-length beyond. They were beginning the sixty-eighth, and Massimo came up behind him in the streets of the lower town. Richard's Ferrari hopped on the rough paving and he slid through the last corner before the run down to the water splash, and in that fraction of a second, Massimo came through into third place. The four cars howled across the creek crossing and zoomed up the mountain, but Von Lutzow was riding the crown of the road so that there was not room to pass even if the following cars had the speed. There wasn't room, but Massimo did it. He ran his left wheels on the grass bordering the ditch until he was past the Maserati and alongside the GRP; only then did Von Lutzow seem aware of him and grant a little bit more of the road. They went for the left-hand corner together and neither would yield. Hans, on the outside, had to go wide; straw bales flew in the air. Massimo held the tight radius of the turn, and they went down the straight still even. One of the spinning bales bounced on the road in front of the Maserati, and Amadeo skidded wildly to avoid it, letting Richard through in the confusion.

Now he was running third, with only two laps to go. Tearing along the straight, he prayed that the machinery would hold together for another five minutes, because he was going to have to thrash it on the sixty-ninth lap.

Passing the stands, Massimo and Von Lutzow were neck and neck, and Richard was aware without looking that the crowds were on their toes, shrieking with excitement.

Massimo delayed braking just long enough to make the castle corner first. The German tucked in behind him, with Richard only a length away. Before they left the lower town, he knew that Massimo was in trouble. Number One no longer behaved as though it was under the control of a master. It took the right-angle corners erratically. For an instant, Richard had a clear view, and he could see that Massimo was hunched over the wheel, trying not to cough.

In the same instant, Richard knew what he was going to do. He was going to harass Von Lutzow and keep him so busy the German would forget all about Massimo. The engine howled in protest as Richard shot down across the water splash, but he came alongside Von Lutzow and pulled to the right until their wheels were nearly touching, forcing him to move over. Von Lutzow yelled something at him in alarm, but he gave way, letting up on the throttle for a moment in his fright. It was a rough thing to do, but Richard was within his rights in doing it; he shot through into second place, and he had saved Massimo for a little longer.

Nevertheless, it had been expensive. He had bent something in revving the engine so high, and on the long flat section through the curving flank of Monti di Beleri he was not getting as much power as before. But neither could the GRP be as healthy as it had been. Von Lutzow was almost level, but could not quite seem to pass.

Richard had his hands full in the hairpin, and then in the chute the German made a desperate effort and got by. All three went over the bridge in a very loose-jointed fashion that gave blunt evidence to the extreme fatigue of the machines and the men.

As he skittered past the building and turned into the street leading to the piazza, Richard risked a backward glance. The Maserati was in the air over the bridge, and Geoffrey and the Gordini were passing and repassing as they flew down the chute. It was still anybody's race, but Richard promised himself that it was going to be his.

The starter showed the flag to signal the last lap, and they went past him three abreast, but Richard was on the outside and had to back off or run down the escape road to the valley. Then Von Lutzow yielded, and Massimo barely got around the turn. Even over the scream of the engines, Richard could hear the roar of the crowd.

Now Massimo looked a little steadier. By the time they were out of the lower town, he was driving with all his old fire, and Von Lutzow couldn't take him. Again on the climb, Richard pressed in on Von Lutzow, but this time Hans would not give way, and so it was Richard who was running with his left wheels on the thin edge of nothing, until he had to back off for the top turn.

On the Mountain Straight for the last time, Massimo crouched so low he was almost invisible in the lead car. Von Lutzow's GRP slipstreamed him for half the distance and then swung out to pass, but there wasn't a mile-an-hour difference between them at full speed on the level. Hans could not overtake. They approached the hairpin at an impossible speed.

When it already seemed too late, smoke poured from the GRP's brakes, and an instant later from Massimo's, and the Ferrari was drifting into the turn in the lead. He was too fast and the drift broke into a broadslide. Massimo overcorrected and the nose swung back through ninety degrees, but he caught it and steadied in a series of small slides. To avoid a crash, Von Lutzow steered sharply to the left, and finding the road already blocked there by the Ferrari, steered right and spun completely around, and stalled. Richard went through, past the revolving GRP, and found himself overtaking Massimo with ease. Drawing alongside, he looked at Massimo. The bandage over his mouth was spattered with oil. Then Richard saw that it was not oil, and that Massimo was only holding himself erect by his grip on the steering wheel.

"Stop!" he yelled at Massimo. "Stop!"

Massimo didn't even hear him. He was accelerating toward the chute, and Richard eased up enough to stay abreast throwing a frantic look behind. Von Lutzow was still stalled broadside in the curve, blocking the road— Geoffrey and the Maserati and the Gordini were all making crash stops. It would not take long to clear the jam, because it was all downhill from there, and easy to restart by coasting.

For a moment Richard thought, It's in the bag—Massimo is wild now, and I can beat him into the chute and over the bridge, and the race is mine . . . but even as he thought it he knew he did not want a victory won from Massimo; he further knew that it was not the victory that was important any more, but only that he had tried hard enough —believing hard enough—so that he had made the victory possible. Understanding that, he was satisfied and he would see to it that Massimo won. It was Massimo's last race—

at least for a long time—because they would take him away
to a hospital, and this would be something for him to remember in the long time he would be an invalid. Richard
held his throttle setting and watched Number One slowly
pull ahead. Massimo could not know that Richard had
anything in reserve, and he was still trying with everything he had.

They turned down into the chute, and Richard had a
moment to think, I don't know where Felice is, but we're
giving Angelo a one-two finish, which is at least the best
two-thirds of what he asked. Massimo's car began to wan-
der, going into the S-bend. Richard's throat contracted in
alarm, but Number One straightened out sharply and
plunged fast for the bridge.

The lead Ferrari went into the drift, onto the bridge,
but something was wrong. Closing up, Richard saw Massimo's head jerking downward as if on a string, and the
drift began to turn into a skid as the machine went into
the air. Busy himself, Richard caught only a slow-motion,
fragmentary picture of what was happening. Number One
landed hard, lopsided, and spun around and slammed
broadside into the straw bales with such force that it rolled
up on the bales on its side and hung there an endless
second. Then it fell back down on its wheels with a great
crash, bouncing several times, Massimo flopping like a rag
doll in the cockpit. Richard, seeing it, himself in the air
over the bridge, knowing that he could not expect to clear
Number One, felt his own machine land, and instead of
trying to continue in the direction he was pointed, turned
straight into the drift, found traction, and steered into the
building on an angle. A straw bale came right over the
hood of the car and almost knocked his head off, but
the nose caromed to the left, and he was able to bring the
car to a halt by the corner of the building. Leaving the
engine running, Richard climbed out and ran back to Massimo.

The crowd was trying to break through the police lines,
and the *carabinieri* were threatening to use clubs on anyone who came out on the course. In a nightmare haze,
Richard saw that the mask had been ripped away from
Massimo's face; he lay against the steering wheel with his
eyes closed, and his fingers were still locked on the rim.
Richard knelt beside him, ripping the glove off his good
hand, to reach into the cockpit and feel for a heartbeat.

Kneeling there, he heard the machines making the screaming turn into the head of the chute. He straightened up, intending to sprint for his own car and get it down into the piazza and across the finish line. But instead of that, he lifted Massimo back from the wheel with one hand, and put all his strength into pushing the Ferrari with the other. It would not move, and he remembered the gear lever. Reaching into the cockpit again, he snapped the lever into neutral, and heaved against the car once more. It began to roll.

The other cars were in the S-bend now, but there might still be time. Marshals were running out to clear the straw bales scattered across the bridge exit, and the flag marshal at the far end of the bridge was waving the orange flag frantically. Richard put every ounce of his weight and strength into the task; he steered Number One around the corner, and headed it down into the piazza. Now he had to trot alongside, steering with his left hand and supporting Massimo with his right. Behind him he heard the first of the cars bouncing over the bridge.

Ahead, the starter was waiting perplexed with the checkered flag, and officials were running toward the finish line from all directions. He looked for Angelo, and waved violently at him, and Angelo ran out from the pit into the path of the slowly approaching Number One, and then ran backwards, staying ten yards ahead of it.

Two lengths from the broad white line, Richard let go.

The Ferrari coasted quietly down the cobbled stretch, and now the piazza was full of the reverberating roar of racing engines behind Richard.

Massimo still sat upright as he crossed the line and took the checkered flag, and in the next instant Von Lutzow flashed across, and then the Maserati and Geoffrey, but it no longer mattered. They had not been able to beat Massimo.

Angelo caught the car just beyond the finish, and Massimo toppled slowly forward like a man dozing in his chair. There was a flash of white that was Ghita, running, and the white of the moving ambulance, and the white of the doctor's coats, and then for a moment the whole world turned white, and Richard knelt down on the cobbles— the crowd pressing past him with a high wailing note—and gave himself up to nausea. . . .

Then Angelo came to him, and led him to the pit, where he had a bottle of cognac.

"We had to pry his hands off the wheel," Angelo said. "He was dead when we lifted him out. I will never ask you anything, Ricardo."

Richard said, "He couldn't restart. He asked me to push. All the way to the line he kept saying: 'Faster—faster, monster.'" He turned away suddenly and the tears ran down his dirty face, making little light-colored channels.

"No one will ever ask," Angelo said softly. "You are a very nice guy, *Ricardo mio,* and one hell of a racing driver."

"Give me the bottle," Richard said.

Angelo shook his head. "The poor little guy."

Richard looked at him, and thought: *Oh, Angelo, if you think that, how little you knew him.*

In the twilight, the last of the racing vans went down the mountain toward the valley. The death of Massimo hung over the village like a pall. It stopped the festival, it canceled the presentation ceremonies. The people were stunned and silent, and already in the fading light the mourning badges were appearing on the doors of the houses, for Massimo belonged to them all.

Richard climbed the long stone stairway. The door was open, and Ghita was kneeling before the plaster figure of the Virgin. He waited outside for a long time in the gathering dusk, and then she stood up and turned.

Her eyes were dry and calm. He went inside, and the room seemed very empty, and he realized that he had never seen this bed before without Massimo in it. The absence of Massimo was stronger than his presence had ever been.

"I must go down the mountain tonight," Richard said.

"But thee will come back?"

"Yes. For the funeral. And for thee."

"I do not hold thee to it, Ricardo," she said.

"It is my wish," Richard said. "It is perhaps too early to speak of these things, but I hope that it will become thy wish, too."

Ghita said, "It is too early for some things, but not for this. I wish to go with thee."

"There are many things to be arranged, so I go to Rome,

to the American embassy, to commence the formalities for thee. I will return in time on Wednesday."

"As thee says."

They stood separate, and he had a fleeting moment of wonder whether it was always to be like this. He would have to be very careful with her, not asking more than she was prepared to give, and eventually it might be all right.

"I had better go now."

She said nothing, only watching him with that gravity that made him feel awkward; it was as though she was comforting him, and offering him her strength. To reassure himself, Richard went to her and put his big hands on her shoulders. She trembled a little under his touch.

"I don't like to leave thee now, but I must."

"Thee is afraid of something?"

"No," he said.

"Thee is afraid that I will not be much good for thee." She watched him, and then added, "Thee fears the memory of Massimo?"

"Perhaps. It's natural."

"Why," she said, "does thee think I wish to go with thee?"

"He wanted you to," Richard said in confusion.

"Already thee has forgotten what I said at the castle."

"That thee has always loved Massimo and nothing would ever change it . . ."

"That there are different loves, Ricardo."

"Yes, but—"

"Go to Rome," she said gently, "and do all thy work, and come back when thee can, and I will be waiting."

There was a singing inside him, so loud that he thought she must be aware of it too, and he tried to stifle it because he was still too caught in the convention of the moment, but it would not be muted. He bent a little and kissed Ghita on the lips.

"*Ciao, Ghita.*"

"*Ciao, Ricardo.*"

He looked at her for a long moment, and then he went out of the house and down the stairway. He did not look back, but he was sure that she was at the window.

THE END
of a novel by
ROBERT SPAFFORD